The mustached man advanced, his tongue moistening his lips. Jessie tried twisting away, but his muscular hands promptly seized her, catching both of her wrists and wrestling her into submission. Then he stepped back, leering with the others as the lamplight threw into relief her tied hands and naked flesh.

"Polhaus, I warn you," Jessie said with bitter ferocity, "you'd best kill me now, for I swear I'll kill you if you don't."

Polhaus sneered and tossed her derringer on top of her pile of clothing. "In time, perhaps, I'll kill you. In time..."

WESLEY ELLIS

LONE STAR

AND THE MEXICAN STANDOFF

A JOVE BOOK

LONE STAR AND THE MEXICAN STANDOFF

A Jove Book / published by arrangement with
the author

PRINTING HISTORY
Jove edition/October 1983

ISBN: 0-515-07259-1

PRINTED IN THE UNITED STATES OF AMERICA

LONE STAR

AND THE
MEXICAN STANDOFF

Chapter 1

Through the blazing heat of the late-summer after-
noon, the Southern Pacific train churned westward
across the grassy slopes, stony plateaus, and low scrub
hills of southern New Mexico. The diamond-stack 4-
4-0 Cooke locomotive surged into a twisty patch of
scarps and gullies, while the sun, continuing its slow
descent, burnished the ten-car bobtail haul of flats,
boxes, and coaches with slanting rays. Soon the track
straightened as the terrain broadened into a series of
low undulations, like a corrugated plain stretching
aridly toward the distant Florida Peak. But instead of
increasing speed, the engineer gradually cut steam and
braked, tugging on the whistle cord to signal the approach of a station.

When the conductor came through the daycoach
calling, "Mosquero! Nex' stop, Mosquero," Victor
Harrigan rose and stretched his cramped legs. "None
too soon," he sighed. "We're a good two hours late."

"And two pounds heavier with dust and soot," Jessica Starbuck added wearily, easing across from the
window seat to stand beside him. "I would've liked
to freshen up first, but now there's not enough time
before our dinner meeting with Señor De Baca. Drat
the luck!"

Nodding, Harrigan took his small gladstone and
Jessica's leather bellows case down from the overhead
rack. Then, with a friendly smile at Ki, who was

1

sliding out from the seat in front, he led the way down the aisle, maneuvering the two bags with the swaying of the carriage.

Victor Harrigan had a rough-hewn body, still spare and hard even though he was in his late thirties. Long-limbed and thick-boned he was, and his clean-shaven face was deeply weathered, with thin lips, a stolid jawline, somber gray eyes, and a slightly fist-bent nose. His features marked him for a saddleman; by contrast, his dark cassimere suit, string tie, and low-heeled boots were the clothes of an urban dweller, of perhaps a minor executive or bureaucrat.

In truth, Harrigan was of both range and town. A moderately successful rancher, he'd joined the territorial government after the last election, and was now down from Santa Fe as an official representative of the current administration. The combination of man and garb was nonetheless startling, appearing peculiarly out of place in this backcountry region. Perhaps that was why curious eyes followed the three as they walked back toward the rear platform.

Or possibly the eyes were focusing on Jessica, the men admiring and the women envious of her striking beauty. Still in her twenties and heiress to the immense Starbuck empire, she moved with lithe, regal grace, her taut, full breasts swelling her stylish two-piece outfit of powder-blue Venetian wool cloth. Her Italian leghorn hat hid the coils of her copper-blond tresses; but the hat's wide brim did little to conceal her cameo face with its pert nose, dimpled chin, and audacious green eyes. She had the milky complexion that some-times goes with hair of that particular deep, rich hue.

Equally intriguing was Ki. Born of a Japanese woman wedded to an American sailor, Ki was the handsome best of two worlds—tall, lean, bronze-skinned, with blue-black straight hair, a strongly boned face, and almond eyes that held a vital intensity, suggesting that here was a man to be reckoned with. Latent power lay in Ki's relaxed yet iron-hard body; and though he didn't pack a firearm, in the vest and pockets of his traveling suit were secreted short daggers and other small throwing weapons—including a supply of *shuriken,* little razor-sharp steel disks shaped like six-pointed stars.

If the trio noticed the stares, they gave no indication. They stepped out onto the platform, where they waited with four other passengers while the train continued slowing and the first shacks flashed by.

Mosquero lay in a flat crescent of land, a wide dry wash curving around it on one edge, and a scattering of cottonwoods, the main wagon road, and the paralleling railroad tracks on the other. It was the largest settlement between Las Cruces and Deming, on the opposite side of the Florida Mountains, and a secondary trail angled from here southeast some sixty miles to Ciudad Juarez, Mexico. But mainly the town was the center of the area by virtue of the Southern Pacific, which, just within the year, had completed its line from Yuma to a new eastern terminus at El Paso. The result was a split community of old adobe dwellings clustered around the original sleepy plaza, and fresh clapboard buildings sprouting near the recently built depot; and of a divergent mix of laborers and peons, gandy dancers and gamblers, Mexicans, Anglos, Indians, and *mestizos* all usually working and sometimes brawling in the heady boomtown atmosphere.

The whistle blew again and the bell began to clang.

The train clattered past loading pens and corrals, then past a small yard of spurs and sidings, on which were parked empty rolling stock and a battered 0-4-0 saddletank switch engine. Crawling now, they chuffed down the center of Mosquero's main street, past Rowland's Emporium . . . the Gilded Lily Saloon . . . a false-fronted feed store . . . the cobbler, gunsmith, and barbershop . . . the locomotive belching steam as it finally lurched to a halt along the cindered apron fronting the peak-roofed depot.

Bystanders and travelers milled about on the platform. The stationmaster emerged, lugging a sack of mail, while his freight handlers began opening the baggage cars and boxcars. Again the three waited patiently as the four passengers before them shuttled themselves and their luggage down the steep platform steps.

At last Harrigan could descend. He paused at the bottom, extending a hand to help Jessica, while Ki stood behind her, holding the iron railing. Something made Ki shift and crane his neck out over the platform.

It wasn't anything tangible at first, merely an anxious feeling. The westering sun flamed off windows and trackside cinders, billowing in heat waves and almost blinding Ki as he gazed, squinting, in careful study. Then he caught it—the extra-bright glint of light reflecting off something long and metallic sticking out from the depot's rooftop cupola.

"Look out!" Ki shouted, and shouldering Jessie roughly back under the protection of the platform overhang, he dove at Harrigan.

A rifle barked twice in quick-levered succession, lead snapping past and ricocheting off the coach's carriage trucks, as Ki threw himself and Harrigan

4

tumbling to the ground. He had a fleeting glimpse of Jessie plunging forward to the railing again, digging into her Chatelaine purse for the custom .38 Colt revolver she carried there.

"Ki! On your left!" came her desperate yell. "Roll!"

Ki rolled, glimpsing a bearded man charging along the cinder bed, leveling a large-caliber pistol. One arm holding Harrigan flat, shielding him as much as possible with his own body, Ki used his free hand to whip out one of his throwing daggers from inside his suit jacket. He threw it instinctively in one sweeping move, a fraction of a second before the man fired. The pistol's discharge reverberated between the depot and the railroad coach, blending with panicked screams and the viscid sound, close by, of a bullet drilling meat.

Harrigan jerked spasmodically. "I'm hit!" he gasped.

Pandemonium was erupting all around them, people shrieking and running, the man who'd fired pivoting to escape in the tumult. But Ki's knife was buried to its hilt in the man's brisket, and after a couple of steps he bent double, took another stride, then dropped to the weeds alongside the cinder bed.

Ki rose to a crouch, to see how badly Harrigan had been wounded. The sniper in the cupola opened up again, slugs splintering the wood of the coach and whining off the rails and the metal undercarriage.

By now Jessie had her .38 out. She hesitated only a moment, then hammered a pair of shots as fast as she could draw a bead on the cupola. Her first slug shattered the window pane above the ambusher's head; her second punctured his skull between his right eye and temple. The man fell from sight, his rifle dropping out the window and skittering down the roof, falling to the depot's freight deck below.

Even before the rifle had landed, Ki was swiveling around to examine Harrigan. Travelers, train crew, and bystanders crowded near, talking excitedly. Some clustered around the coach platform, while others bunched around the man Ki had knifed, both groups abruptly drawing aside as the sheriff elbowed his way through.

Lean-hipped, wide-shouldered, a tarnished star pinned to his rumpled plaid vest, the sheriff had dull white hair and an angry flush to his lined face. Behind him came another badge-toter, a youngish deputy with the same wedge-shaped build as the sheriff, wearing bib overalls and a determined scowl. His scowl was mostly directed at a third man who was dogging their boots—a man big in height, stance, and girth, richer living than a lawman's having padded his gut until his sateen shirt no longer wrinkled at the grab of his belt.

All of this Ki saw peripherally, while he was ripping open the seam of Harrigan's left trouser leg. "You should've lain still and not kicked out, Victor," Ki said with mock exasperation. "Now you've got a nice neat hole through your calf."

"I'm alive, so I guess I don't have any more kick coming," Harrigan quipped, though his voice was thin with pain.

"What happened?" the sheriff demanded.

"A couple of killers tried to bushwhack us," Jessica answered, hastily replacing her revolver in her purse and stepping down from the platform. "That man over there, and a second one up in the cupola," she added, then raised her skirt hem to begin tearing off a strip

6

of her lace-trimmed petticoat. When she glimpsed the sheriff's disapproval, she snapped impatiently, "You want him to bleed to death?"

"No, ah, but—"

"The work of them damned Mexican bandits!" the man next to the deputy growled loudly, his voice rasping like sandpaper on wood, and there were angry mutters of assent from the surrounding crowd. "Something's got to be done about that coyote Renegado and his cutthroat gang!"

"Wal, do it after m' train leaves," the stationmaster interjected irascibly. "Hellfire, we're behind schedule as it is!"

The sheriff glowered. "'Tain't right, Dugan, putting the railroad above flesh an' blood, but okay, pull out." He turned to his deputy. "Flynn, toss these folks' bags off'n the platform, and then go wake up McHugh. He's about due to go on duty, anyhow." The sheriff next pointed to two burly loiterers. "You, and you there, take that man's body over to Doc Scofield's, and send him over here, pronto."

"Not here," Jessica spoke up tartly, from where she crouched by Harrigan, bandaging his wound with swift efficiency. "We're all registered at the Mirador, wherever that is. We'll take him there."

"The hotel's just on t'other side of the station," the sheriff explained. "Not far atall . . . but mayhaps we should fetch a stretcher?"

Harrigan said, "Forget it, I'll make it in a breeze." He clenched his teeth, shuddering, while Jessica finished stanching the blood flow, indifferent to the ruin of her expensive, tailor-made outfit.

Ki, meanwhile, had moved to help Deputy Flynn remove their luggage from the platform. He paused

7

as the sheriff's grudging "volunteers" passed, carting the limp corpse by its arms and legs. Studying the dead ambusher, Ki saw through the thick mustache and beard and sunbaked appearance of the skin, and recognized him for what he was: an Anglo, not a Mexican. It made him wonder, as he heard the florid man who'd arrived with the sheriff and deputy continue his tirade.

"Mad-dog greasers! Only thing they understand is rope an' lead! You can't deal with 'em, I keep telling you, and this here's proof!"

"Proves nothing," the sheriff replied harshly. "Some Mexicans are bad, but most're good, August, which is true about any slice of life."

"Listen here, Ballard!" a voice called from the crowd. "Maybe you're sheriff, but maybe Polhaus is right! Maybe we gotta get tough and start carin' for our own skins. What do you say, mister?"

The question was addressed to Ki, who, as one of the intended victims, would be most likely to agree to swift and violent retribution.

"I think we've got to stop the renegades," Ki replied evenly. "But I also think you'd better go check the dead man, because he's no more Mexican than you or me."

For the moment that seemed to silence August Polhaus and his backers. He and Sheriff Ballard were not friends, Jessica sensed, though they were well acquainted. She straightened and stepped aside as Ki, leaving their bags trackside, moved in to lift Harrigan gently upright, balancing his weight in a lifesaver's hold, an arm about his waist.

The sheriff thrust his shoulder beneath Harrigan's other armpit, and between Ki and himself they were

8

able to support Harrigan as he slackened, legs buckling. While the crowd began to break and drift apart, and the stationmaster herded passengers aboard the train, the two strong men slowly and awkwardly shuffled Harrigan toward the depot and the hotel beyond.

"August Polhaus is a strongly opinionated hothead," Sheriff Ballard explained to Jessica on the way. "He's lost considerable stock to Renegado's band, being the leading rancher in these parts, and he's fed up with the raids and massacres. We all are, but that don't mean we should cotton to his vigilante notions. That ain't the law, by gum!"

No, it certainly was not, Jessica agreed grimly. Worse, it was the potential spark that could ignite the tinderbox this border region had recently become—and that, if allowed to burst into flame, could explode into another war between Mexico and the United States. . . .

Lawlessness had been Jessica's implacable enemy since the death of her father, Alex Starbuck. Most always, her fight had been waged against a wealthy, unscrupulous international crime cartel, of which Alex Starbuck had run afoul while beginning his career in the Orient. His discovery of this Prussian-based ring, whose aim was the control of emerging America, had led to the murder of his wife—Jessica's mother—and eventually to his own assassination. But by then his business had evolved into a far-flung empire of vast resources and influence, and his daughter had grown into a daring and determined young woman. Using her powerful inheritance and her father's secret records, and aided by Ki—who'd immigrated from Japan as a youth, and had virtually grown up with her—Jessica had been continuing the struggle to de-

9

stroy every vestige of the criminal conspiracy.

This time, however, there didn't appear to be any connection between the crime syndicate and the dangerous problem at hand. Yet this was lawlessness nonetheless, lawlessness in a deadly form... and when asked to help, even in a small way, Jessica could not refuse.

Since the first of the year, the Mexican states of Chihuahua and Sonora had been devastated by a guerilla band allegedly dedicated to overthrowing General Porfirio Diaz's government. Its head was a self-proclaimed *revolutionario* calling himself *El Renegado*—The Renegade— and his rallying cry to free Mexico from its tyrannical oppressors was being answered by hundreds of impoverished peons, who were swelling his gang into a ragtag peasant army beyond containment.

Although concerned, the United States would normally refrain from interfering with Mexico's internal strife. Yet, recently, six villages in New Mexico, four in Texas, and two in southeastern Arizona had been attacked, their stores and banks looted and torched, neighboring ranches pillaged, and a total of thirty-eight men, women, and children wantonly butchered. And the marauders, as the few survivors reported, all repeatedly screamed, *"Viva El Renegado!"*

Evidently the Renegaders, as Renegado's force had come to be known, were invading United States territory. In each instance, moreover, the Renegaders did not flee south over the border, but across into New Mexico's desolate Portrillo Mountains. As hard as it was to believe, Renegado seemed to be making his hideout in the United States.

Not surprisingly, the American citizens living along

10

the border strip were up in arms. Already one lynch mob had retaliated by laying waste to a Mexican hamlet and hanging five peasants. Dark rumors of other vigilante groups stringing up innocent Mexican-Americans were circulating, adding to the ferment.

Under pressure, President Hayes had communicated with General Diaz. To show his alarm and his desire for cooperative action, the President had revoked the objectionable order of June 1, 1877, authorizing U.S. troops to cross the border without Mexican permission. Diaz, in turn, had proven receptive to proposals for a U.S.–Mexican expedition. Such a joint venture had worked before, when military of both nations had united against the Apache leader Victorio. Now, however, Mexican nationals were involved, making it a much more sensitive issue; so it was decided that high-level representatives should first meet to determine a basic political strategy for the combined operation.

It was one thing for General Diaz to declare Don Felipe De Baca as special envoy to negotiate on behalf of his government. It was quite another for President Hayes to persuade a balky and somewhat blind Congress to agree. Hayes figured his best choice was to lock House and Senate leaders in a room with Envoy De Baca, and not release them until they'd realized the gravity of the situation. An impossibility, of course—but his second choice was a practical if cynical maneuver.

By happenstance, three influential senators and two congressmen were on a summer junket, ostensibly to investigate how the railroads had used the vast land endowments and loans that Congress had granted them. It was amazing how many miles of track needed inspecting in the hotels, fancy restaurants, and gentlemen's clubs of Omaha, St. Louis, and San Francisco. President Hayes assumed their tour would continue much the same on its return swing through Los Angeles, Tucson, and El Paso; obviously, to arrange talks anywhere that there was entertainment available would be a waste of time, and probably be resented to boot. The only spot to meet would have to be out nowhere— or better yet, aboard a train while traveling through nowhere, with the politicos bored and cornered.

Such as the nowhere between Mosquero and El Paso.

There'd been other reasons for picking Mosquero. It was near the Portrillo Mountains, the base of Renegado's American forays. It was readily accessible to envoy De Baca, who, with his honor guard, had already arrived from Mexico City via the Mexican Central rail link at El Paso—Ciudad Juarez. And it provided the start of a journey long enough for full discussion, yet short enough so that everyone didn't sicken of one another before it was over.

President Hayes had dispatched his Secretary of War to California, where, late the previous month, the congressional party had been forewarned in a very low-key manner before leaving on their special Southern Pacific train. About now, a representative of the Arizona Territory would be boarding the train at Maricopa. The pleasantries would continue. But two days hence, that would all change, when the train stopped in Mosquero for Victor Harrigan and Felipe De Baca.

The only hitch in President Hayes's well-laid plans was the absence of an official Texas representative. Governor Roberts wanted his lieutenant governor to represent the state, but a scheduling conflict prevented the lieutenant-governor's inclusion until the train reached El Paso. So, in his stead, Jessica Starbuck had been requested to join the train as an informal advance representative. She was a personal friend of the governor's, but more than that, her sprawling ranch had been a constant target of Renegado's raids, and her losses were greater than anyone else's in Texas— certainly greater than Polhaus's here in New Mexico. Besides, the presence of a charming, intelligent woman might well dampen any outburst of frayed tempers.

It was hoped that by the time the train arrived in El Paso, the congressional party would have given its seal of approval. It would then continue on back to Washington, and Jessie, accompanied by Ki, would return to her ranch. The Secretary of War, the three representatives, and Don Felipe De Baca would remain behind, hammering out the details of a coordinated assault against the Renegaders.

As politics went, it all appeared relatively simple. The conference should work; it *had* to work, if peace was to be preserved between Mexico and the United States. If matters were left unresolved—or left to narrow-minded bigots like August Polhaus—a flash flood of hatred and reprisal could easily be unleashed, which could ultimately embroil both nations in bloody, unwanted conflict.

The conference, Jessie knew, must not fail. . . .

Chapter 2

The Hotel Mirador was a graceless two-story hulk, with a musty-smelling lobby and a marble-topped counter, behind which were an array of pigeonholes and a clerk. The clerk was a wizened, chinless man with a few wisps of hair combed flat across his skull. He looked up with wide, watery eyes, and when he spoke, his teeth showed yellow and crooked.

"We don't allow no drunks in here, Sheriff, you know that."

"This man ain't drunk, Wilmer." Ballard shrugged his shoulder, shifting Harrigan's cumbersome weight to a better position, and glared coldly at the clerk. "These folks say they've got reservations here."

"Harrigan, Starbuck, and Ki," Jessica declared, beginning to sign the register. "Starbuck and Ki are to have adjoining rooms."

The clerk slapped three big brass keys on the counter. "One-ten and twelve connect, nine's just across the hall. Upstairs. Payment's in advance and checkout time is—Gawd! Blood on m' carpet!"

"Don't faint," the sheriff jeered, as the horrified clerk craned forward to ogle the smeared red drops leading from the front door. "Say...is one of the rooms next to one-oh-nine vacant, by any chance?"

"One-eleven is, but..." The clerk swallowed thickly. "This got anything to do with that shootin' fracas I heard a moment ago?"

14

"Never you mind, Wilmer, you just give one-eleven's key to one or t'other of my deputies when they come in. They're stayin' the night."

"Now hold on! Nobody stays here for free!"

"Two nights, maybe," Jessie cut in crisply, and placed a number of banknotes on the counter. "In advance, all four rooms, all right?"

The clerk nodded sourly, scooping up the money.

The narrow staircase proved painfully difficult for Harrigan to maneuver, no matter how slowly and carefully Ki and the sheriff took each step. Jessie, hesitating on the second-floor landing to look back at their struggles, said sympathetically, "It's very close now."

"Don't worry. I'm no more'n grazed," Harrigan replied gamely, though his face was ashen and his breath was noticeably ragged.

Hastening along the dimly lit corridor to Harrigan's room, Jessie unlocked the door and left it wide while she crossed to draw back the bedspread. Brushing past her, Ki and Sheriff Ballard eased Harrigan down, straightened his feet, and got him stretched out.

Jessie arranged a pillow under his left knee, to lift his wounded leg a little. "That'll have to do until the doctor arrives."

"That'll do plumb dandy," Harrigan responded, grinning weakly yet defiantly. "But it looks like I'll be missing our little meeting."

Jessie nodded. "Ki? Maybe we should telegraph the ranch."

"Good idea." Ki started toward the door.

"Wait, I'll come with you," the sheriff said, then turned to Jessie. "You'll be sticking pat for Doc Scofield, won't you?"

"Oh, yes. And thanks, Sheriff. It's very considerate of you, having one of your deputies stay next door to protect Mr. Harrigan."

"Nope, I'm placin' both my men on tap, and not just for his sake. Cold murder gripes me something fierce. It was a deliberate trap, that I know, but I don't know if another one's fixed to be sprung. That's 'cause I don't know why the last one was set, or which one of you it was supposed to kill."

"Why, there's no possible reason we—"

"Now, now, Miss Starbuck, I recognized your name as soon as you spoke it down in the lobby. Big ranchers make big enemies. And maybe you're with Mr. Harrigan, maybe not; I never heard tell of him afore."

"I'm from the governor's office," Harrigan explained, cautiously skirting details. "We're together, yes, but're only passing through, hoping to visit some, ah, acquaintances we gather are also staying over in town. We're leaving by train, day after tomorrow."

"Sure. Well, excuse my impertinence, but I sorta smell a decayin' rat in the walls." Shaking his head, Ballard stomped to the door. "I guess I better go check that dead gent in the cupola, and see if he's a stranger too. Maybe he'll have more to tell me."

Together, the sheriff and Ki strode down to the lobby and outside. "The telegrapher's aside the depot," the sheriff directed, angling that way. "You wouldn't have any extra to add, would you?"

"I wish I did," Ki replied. "Your Mr. Polhaus was quick to blame the ambush on Renegado, which makes as much sense as anything. Except that the man I killed wasn't Mexican, and Renegado hardly needs any hired help from the States. But I can't think of anyone else."

"Uh-huh, and nobody knew you were stopping in

16

Mosquero, and the whole thing's a complete mystery to you, to all of you." The sheriff grunted, unconvinced, but lapsed into silence until they'd reached the depot and he'd shown Ki the door to the telegrapher's office. "I gotta hold your knife, for whenever a coroner's jury bothers to convene."

Ki shrugged. "Keep it."

"And here I thought it was part of a matched set," Ballard grumped sarcastically and, with a departing nod, walked away.

Ki entered the small office, which was not much more than a windowless shed abutting the depot. Lounging at a large curtain-top desk, the telegrapher was playing a game of solitaire. He glanced up, a bull-necked, carrot-haired man who spoke with an Irish brogue.

"Faith, a coolie in a suit! What can I be doin' for you, m'boy?"

Ki stiffened. He was aware that the telegrapher's insult was meant as a ribbing, that the Irish and the Chinese had scrapped in feisty rivalry ever since the first big railroad construction push in 1863. No, it was being mistaken for a Chinese that was so damned irritating.

Choking down his annoyance, Ki flipped a silver dollar onto the desk. "Can you raise the Circle Star Ranch, Sarah, Texas?"

"For this, I'll raise hell itself." The coin vanished and the telegrapher hunched over his key, clicking it with an experienced touch, and a few moments later the key responded with a rattle of its own. "Line's clear," he then said to Ki. "What's your message?"

In a few terse sentences, Ki dictated the details of their arrival, Harrigan's wounding, and the chance of

17

a delay. He knew that the Starbuck operators would, without needing to be told, relay applicable parts of his message to those concerned, and to nobody else. He didn't know about the telegrapher here, and when he was through, he emphasized, "It's confidential."

"Every wire is, and has been since I started poundin' brass," the telegrapher retorted. "Hold tight, let's see if they got it."

Ki leaned against the edge of the desk, to wait for the Circle Star's acknowledging response. The telegrapher picked up his greasy deck of cards to resume play, and said conversationally, "Didn't catch your blade-toss during the ruckus; I was a mite too late out the door for that. But by the looks o' your target, I fair imagine it was a sweetheart of a throw."

"You don't know who that man was, do you?"

"Not a local, I know. Most likely a Renegader. I mean, I overheard your rebuff of ol' Polhaus, but that don't mean nothin. Plenty o' them polecats are from our side o' the fence."

"Not from Mexico?" Ki leaned closer. "Americans?"

The telegrapher shrugged. "Hard to tell. And perchance I'm muddled, but strike me down if not just last spring, I recall Digger O'Dell traipsin' through here to join up with some brigands."

"A countryman of yours?"

"Certainly not! O'Dell is an Orangeman, and I wouldn't put anything past the likes o' him. Damned if he weren't back within a fortnight, though, swearin' he wasn't gettin' mixed up with no crazy revolters. He told me he'd been campin' with them in some kind of fort in the hills."

"The Portrillos?"

18

"O'Dell was hazy about that. Said he didn't know where he was most o' the time, on account of him being from Boston and not accustomed to our land." The telegrapher riffled the deck and was preparing to turn a card, when the key chattered abruptly. "There y'are, m'boy. Your message has been received and acknowledged."

Figuring he'd little to gain by asking further, and dubious of the story he'd prompted so far, Ki thanked the telegrapher and left.

He started back to the hotel. Dusk was encroaching rapidly now, the waning rays of sunset casting thin, shimmering tendrils along the shadowy main street. The train had long gone, most shops and stores were closed for the day, and the saloons were still preparing for the night. Mosquero lay in that brief, desoltory transition of evening.

Drawing abreast of the little alley between the mercantile store and a small boutique, Ki heard someone whisper, *"Señor!"* He hesitated, peering into the alley, but saw only a hunched outline.

"Señor, adelante!"

"No thanks, you come out here."

"Absolutamente no!" The whisper quivered with fear. Then, in English, "Th-they'll kill me if they see me! Please!"

"Who're 'they'?"

"The hombres who hunt you." There was a pause, the scuffing of a boot, and now Ki could glimpse in the murkiness a bit of a pale checkered shirt. *"Venga rápido, Señor, no puedo esperar!"*

Ki had no intention of going quickly into that alley, and if the unknown silhouette couldn't wait, that was just too damn bad. He slipped his hands into his vest pockets, fingering his *shuriken* nestled there while he surveyed the street around him. A few townsmen were casually strolling, none of them close by, and none appearing to be taking any special interest in him. Every instinct in him warned that the hissing voice was wrong, that its plea was a fake, and yet...

He slid into the dimness. *"Muy bien."*

"Gracias," the man said as the black well of the alley enclosed them. *"Vamos al caso—"* But instead of "getting to the point," there was a slight break in the man's voice, a little catch as though his attention had been momentarily distracted by something else.

Something in back of Ki.

Ki whirled, and glimpsed another man looming over him from out of a concealed side doorway to the mercantile store. The other man had his arm raised high, gripping a butcher knife.

With a sharp twisting of his body to the left, Ki threw a right-forearm block to deflect the slashing blade, and countered by ramming the heel of his left palm in a *teisho* blow to the man's nose. He saw the brutal features contort with startled pain, and heard the satisfying sound of cartilage splitting. The man's head flew back, striking the doorway, shards of fractured nasal bone spearing up into his brain. His honed steel blade sliced past the corded muscles of Ki's belly, snagging his suit jacket slightly, then arching harmlessly to land in the dirt.

Dead on his feet, the man began crumpling. Ki was already pivoting back to the first man, following through with a catlike shift to deliver a disabling *mae-geri-keage*—a forward snap-kick. Too late. Running footfalls were retreating down the alley, and he realized that the man had started to flee even before he'd seen his partner die.

"*Jesús!*" the man was howling in the distance. "*Dios mio!*"

Ki stood in angry silence, staring at the darkness into which the man had disappeared. Then, turning, he knelt to examine the knifer, who was slumped as if asleep against the mercantile wall. He was Mexican. The one who'd lured him into the alley was unquestionably Mexican also, but beyond that meager fact, Ki knew no more than before.

Sighing, Ki straightened and walked out of the alley. His well-trained defensive reflexes had once again reacted swiftly and exactly, which was always comforting but sometimes annoying, especially when the need for information was so great. The confrontation had also been so fast, so quiet, that apparently it had passed unnoticed. Nobody was shouting alarm, nobody was coming on the double to see what was wrong; it was almost as if he'd never stepped into the alley at all.

Ki left it that way as he headed toward the hotel again. He'd tell Jessie, and would notify Sheriff Ballard in due course, but otherwise he felt no compulsion to call attention to the corpse. On the contrary, this had been a day of violence thus far, and fear was strong in Mosquero. Noise of a second attack so soon would breed more of the kind of talk that Mexico and the United States were trying to curtail. It could only lead to stirring up otherwise reasonable folks into rampaging around, ready to pepper holes in anybody who so much as sneezed in Spanish. So let the knifer stay there until morning, or until the sheriff disposed of him discreetly; there was no reason to allow him to do more harm dead than he had done while alive. . . .

When Ki arrived back at the room, Dr. Scofield was just finishing his adjustments of the fresh bandage encircling Harrigan's wounded leg. Jessica was by the window, having cracked its sash to air out the pungent odor of antiseptic, and seeing Ki enter, she greeted him: "Was that you making all the racket outside just now?"

"No, that was the deputies," Ki responded. "When I passed their room, they came barging into the hall like rogue buffaloes."

Crossing, he spotted Harrigan's gladstone bag and added, "They remembered our luggage, too." And then he smiled at Harrigan. "How are you feeling?"

"Tired." Harrigan was undressed and under the covers, and he sighed wanly when the doctor tucked his leg in. "Funny how a tiny piece of lead can tire a man worse'n riding drag on a cattle drive."

"Small wonder, you've lost a lot of blood," the doctor said, packing his satchel. "I'll have the desk clerk fetch you a big steak dinner and a dose of whiskey. Best cure known for pumping it back in you."

"Thanks—"

"Don't thank me yet, not before you see my bill. Ain't often I get patients I can charge full-bore." Scofield, bald and butterball-plump, waddled to the door. "I'll stop by tomorrow morning." He shut the door, and a second later there was a commotion as his deputies, Flynn and McHugh, tumbled out from their room to intercept him.

"Ballard's got a sharp crew," Ki commented.

Harrigan chuckled, then regarded both Jessie and

22

Ki with somber directness. "Y'know, I'm in your debt more'n I'm in the doc's."

Jessie shook her head. "Don't thank us either, Victor."

"I would've bled to death or been killed if you two—"

"We did what anyone would've done."

"Point is, the anyone was you," he persisted, grimacing as he tried to sit up. He saw affectionate concern growing deeper in Jessie's eyes, and for his part, he felt a stirring of impulses long forgotten. The unattached women of his world were frontier girls sapped of their youth by drudgery, or society maidens inflated by vanity and self-indulgence. Jessie had escaped both fates, and there was something about her that suggested she'd managed to do so on her own, and would have even if she'd been born destitute. The Starbuck millions be damned; she was a smart, mature, independent woman who'd not lost her youthful charms. Her rare sensuality attracted him more than he, a confirmed bachelor, cared to admit. Gruffly he said, "Enough of this. You should be on your way to meet De Baca."

Jessica pursed her lips. "I don't like leaving you alone."

"Alone? With those eager beavers next door, just rarin' to come to the rescue if I more'n belch in my sleep? Besides, you heard the doc. Nothing wrong with me that rest, meat, and booze won't fix."

"All right, if you insist. I won't feel easy, though, until we've put you safely aboard the train and we're on our way to El Paso."

"Nor I, truth to tell," Harrigan admitted, then smiled

23

faintly. "Give my regards and regrets to De Baca, Jessica. We'll worry later. If trouble's still brewing, it won't be boiling over here tonight."

Ki thought of the attack in the alley, but kept mum as he and Jessie left the room. The deputies immediately wrenched open their door to check who was in the corridor, and Flynn said, "Whups, sorry."

"Don't apologize for doing your job," Jessie replied. "We'll be gone a short time, at La Posada Duquesa. How do we reach it?"

McHugh gave directions. He was slightly broader and older than Flynn, with the look of hard experience about him. Both impressed Jessie as they had Ki, as being competent, honest, tenacious lawmen. "The inn is close by, you can't miss it," McHugh finished, "but it's part of our old town. Mayhaps one of us should go along with you."

Jessie shook her head. "We're expected, and we'll have plenty of protection. No, it's Mr. Harrigan who needs guarding, if anyone does."

She and Ki continued on down to the lobby. Behind the marble-countered desk, the clerk paused while stuffing messages in the bank of pigeonholes, and snapped, "Room service is an extra charge."

Jessie flung a couple more banknotes on the counter. "This should settle Mr. Harrigan's dinner and refreshments." As she swept by to the door, Ki glanced coldly at the clerk and added, "If he lacks for anything, at any time, I'll settle with you personally."

They began walking toward the original quarter of Mosquero. A faint scent of dust lingered in the warm air, as, along the main street, the night's activities were stirring with life. Soon the clapboard structures ended, to be replaced by squat adobes with protruding, weathered *vigas* and earth-coated thatch roofs. They entered the old plaza while, tersely, Ki related what had happened to him in the alley.

"I'm shocked, but not surprised," Jessica responded as they walked around the central well. "Renegado has publicly threatened to kill all in his way, and obviously he figures that includes us."

"I suppose I should've told the deputies, if not Harrigan."

"No, then one of them would've had to leave to investigate it, and I much prefer having both of them stay right where they are."

"I'd prefer having both of them stay in the same room with Harrigan," Ki said, his features hardening. "Let's make this a quick visit, Jessica. I've got a feeling that something's about to pop."

They turned on to a brick path that led to the galleried porch of a whitewashed, stucco-fronted building. A carved sign atop the porch overhang read LA POSADA DUQUESA. This was Mosquero's other hotel, the one catering to those of a more Mexican persuasion, so naturally this was where Envoy De Baca and his guard had chosen to lodge.

Inside, its tiled foyer was cooler, cozier, and patently cleaner than the Mirador's lobby. On both sides were wide arches, the one on the right connecting to a small dining hall, the one on the left leading to a center courtyard enclosed by a series of rooms. At the rear was a counter, unattended, and a bead-curtained doorway from which filtered the clatter and babble of a kitchen crew.

Noisier still was the dining room, which echoed with the sounds of hearty conversation and feasting. Jessie and Ki crossed and glanced in.

Seated at the head of a food-laden table was Don Felipe De Baca. It had to be him, of that they were convinced, even though they'd never laid eyes on so much as a picture of him. He exuded the very essence of a distinguished grandee in his late fifties, Castilian of feature, patrician of manner, leonine with silver hair and vandyke mustache and goatee. As befit his station, he was resplendent in a black silk cutaway, a black vest, and a black cravat with a pinkish pearl tie pin. A starburst medallion hung from his neck and gleamed in the room's dim lamplight.

Six other men, lined up three to each side of De Baca, were equally identifiable as junior officers of the Mexican military. They wore parade uniforms festooned with gold braid and brass buttons, and carried sidearms in buttoned holsters, as well as dress swords in ornate scabbards. Their faces looked rosily flushed and damp, possibly from the heat, from their stifling uniforms, or from overindulgence in wine—or, most likely, from a combination of all three.

De Baca, noticing Jessie and Ki by the archway, called out to them. *"Deseaba usted algo?"* he demanded, frowning, while his companions quieted to stare with him at the intruders.

"Siento molestarle," Jessie replied, apologizing for having disturbed him. Entering, she introduced Ki and herself, and explained why they were late and why Señor Harrigan was unable to attend.

"Oíga!" De Baca gasped after listening to her, then switched to English. "I'm deeply saddened to hear of such misfortune. But now that you're here, come join us. We're just having our dessert."

"Thank you, I'm afraid not. We must be getting back."

26

"Please, I insist!" De Baca raised the brandy snifter he held in his right hand. "If not for dessert, then at least for a small libation, a toast to future good luck and the success of our mission."

"We can scarcely decline that," Jessie allowed, knowing that to do so would be unforgivably rude. She and Ki took chairs at the end of the table and sat, smiling at De Baca. "We accept with pleasure."

"*Bueno!*" As a decanter and two snifters were passed down, De Baca grinned broadly, adding, "And a special toast to beauty, *compadres*, to radiance personified, brightening our drab table."

De Baca's six guards nodded and grinned on cue, though they probably didn't understand his words. Jessie could have done without his compliments in any language, but she remained smiling, disguising her irritation at such overblown flattery. Ki's smile turned tight and sardonic; he respected some men but bowed to none, and scorned the way these guards toadied and fawned before the Mexican envoy.

"I'd been told of the affair at the depot, but not of your involvement," De Baca continued, serious again. "*Our* involvement, I should say. Unquestionably, Señor Harrigan is the victim, perhaps merely the first, of Renegado's drive to destroy our conference."

"You're assuming that Renegado's found out about it, yet as far as I know, all the preparations have been kept strictly confidential."

"A state secret is a contradiction in terms, Señorita Starbuck, and two governments are privy to this one. How Renegado learned is not important; that he *has* learned is discomfiting. It's placed everyone concerned in grave jeopardy. Distressing, most distressing . . . but one hurdle at a time, eh? Tell me, precisely what is the condition of Señor Harrigan?"

"We left him resting comfortably. He has a clean wound, no bone damage, and simply needs to take it easy and let it mend."

"Will he be recovered sufficiently to travel with us?"

"I imagine so, though we can't be sure until then." Jessie sipped her brandy. "If I'm any judge of Victor Harrigan, he'll fight to board the train, no matter how bad off he is. Your men may have to help us rope him to his bed."

De Baca chuckled. "Consider them at your service, Señorita."

In that moment, with no warning whatever, the rear service door between the kitchen and dining hall burst open. Heavily armed men poured in, forming a crescent around the head of the table.

Ki lunged from his chair, reaching into his vest pockets, while Jessie reached into her purse for her custom .38 revolver. The Mexican honor guard were also groping for their holstered pistols, but all of them froze before they'd completed their draws. Reason overcame reflex, in the face of leveled carbine repeaters, and the brusque command from one of the invaders:

"Do not move, *crétinos,* not if you value your worthless hides! Hold, and be silent before the warriors of the mighty El Renegado!"

Chapter 3

Coldly, Jessie studied the Renegaders, counting seven of them, three in soiled white peons' clothes, and four in scruffy trail garb. A few wore wide-brimmed sombreros, some had bandoliers strung diagonally across their chests, and most were filthy and heavily bearded. Motley or not, they all fingered triggers like the finest of warriors.

"What's the meaning of this?" De Baca had scraped back his chair and, unlike his rigidly motionless guardsmen, was defiantly rising to his full height. "How dare you! Leave at once!"

"Deja de ladrar—stop yapping!" commanded the one who'd spoken before. He was squat, barrel-chested, and wore a murderous expression. "Fernando! Pepe! Take the *Federalisto* to the horses."

Instantly, two Renegaders jumped forward and seized De Baca. He wrestled furiously in their grip, yelling, "Help! *Socorro!"* until a dirty palm clamped over his mouth and almost suffocated him.

Nobody could aid De Baca; it would have been suicidal to try. His honor guard stirred restively, stymied, their hands held high and quivering with angry frustration. Jessie sat apparently resigned and weaponless; her hands were folded atop her open purse, her left concealing the bulge of her revolver, her right poised to dart in after it. Ki, too, seemingly accepted the futility of resistance, standing loose-limbed, his

29

thumbs hooked casually in his vest pockets.

Despite his frantic struggling, De Baca was half-carried, half-dragged through the service doorway. They could hear him thrashing as he was bundled across the kitchen, then the squeaking hinges of a back exit as he was spirited out into the blackness of the night beyond.

The leader of the abducting gang raised his left hand, keeping his well-used Winchester '73 steady in his right. The remaining four men began backing toward the service door, their eyes dark and malevolent. When they were a step from the threshold, they seemed to move side by side, almost imperceptibly, but as if they were maneuvering according to some prearranged plan.

"Adios, amigos," the leader said, his lips parting in an ugly parody of a grin. His carbine lifted slightly in his grasp. . . .

In that instant, exchanging alarmed glances, Jessie and Ki realized what was to happen—realized that the kidnap gang was now a firing squad; that, having successfully swiped the Mexican envoy, the Renegaders were about to show those of lesser importance no quarter. And they knew that however swiftly they drew their weapons—however accurately Ki flung *shuriken* and Jessie fired bullets—they'd never down the line of five men, before the five riddled them and the others.

They also knew they had to try.

Jessie, thrusting her hand in her purse, twisted away, ducking, while Ki abruptly grasped the table's edge and tilted it to send it over. *"Cuidado!"* Jessica was shouting. "Watch out, they're going to—"

Shoot they did, and the rest of her desperate warn-

30

ing was lost in the explosive fusillade of carbines, their point-blank discharges thunderous in the small room. Erupting in aftermath came the blast of Jessie's revolver through the bottom of her purse, the crashing of plates, glasses, and silverware as the table thumped over on its side, and the shrieks and choking groans of agony as the guardsmen spilled, dying, out of their chairs, or clawed for their pistols.

Four Renegaders hastily levered fresh rounds, the fifth looking stupefied at the hole Jessie had punched in his chest. Hurling herself low behind the bulwark of the overturned table, Jessie worked in a frenzy to free her revolver, which had become snagged in her purse. Ki reared from behind cover and, though blinded by the powder smoke, loosed a spray of *shuriken* with quick snaps of his wrist, as if he were dealing the Renegaders a fast round of cards.

A Renegader's gagging cough mingled with the staccato reports of their carbines. Jessie tried to straighten, still tearing at her purse, but Ki pushed her back down, fully expecting to meet a Renegader's slug while he aimed more *shuriken* by the muzzle flashes of the carbines. Two guardsmen gamely returned the fire as well, and a third Renegader dropped, howling, to the floor. Above all the din, Ki thought he recognized the voice of the leader yelling hoarsely:

"Vámonos, muchachos! Ándale! Ándale!"

Only one other Renegader remained alive to escape with the leader. The pair turned and dashed through the service door, leaving in their wake a blood-splattered carnage of nine dead or dying men.

Ki pursued them with a vengeance. Clearing the table, he sprinted the length of the dining hall, dodging bodies and pausing only long enough to retrieve his

31

thrown *shuriken*—except for the one embedded in the throat of the Renegader he'd hit. By then, Jessie had joined him, equally determined to catch up with the last of the Renegaders.

They raced into the kitchen. It was a gory shambles, the cook and crew sprawling with their throats slit, the Renegaders' method of silencing them after sneaking in from the rear of the hotel.

A short, narrow corridor led from the kitchen and through a pantry to a back entrance. They dove along it—when suddenly a black outline took shape in the doorway ahead. Instinctively they flattened against the pantry shelves; gunflame speared into the room a second later, lead blanketing the corridor, ricocheting off adobe walls, shattering crockery and glass jars. Then the figure vanished.

Jessie and Ki chased after the gunman. The lightning-strike difference between reacting instantly and hesitating to think had spared them, just as it had in the dining hall, and at other times in the past. They reached the doorway, hearing the sound of galloping horses, and ran out into a large, bare-earth yard.

Thick summer dust billowed around them, churned up by hooves as the Renegaders spurred their mounts into bolting action. The lung-clogging pall made them little more than silhouettes, wavering like mirages seen through a sandstorm. Jessie slowed, braced her arm, and fired at the retreating shapes. She missed as the riders veered abruptly to avoid a fence of stacked cholla branches. Again she sighted, and her pistol, now free of her purse, bucked in her fist as she squeezed off her final shot.

One of the Renegaders cried out and hunched over in his saddle. As he toppled sideways, his boot caught in the stirrup and he was dragged some twenty yards before his leg jarred loose and he rolled to a halt. Ignoring him, the other Renegaders fled up between a row of brush-covered ramadas and disappeared out across the darkened flats.

Hurrying to the fallen Renegader, Jessie and Ki recognized him as the leader. *"Adios, amigo,"* Ki muttered, remembering how the dead man had smilingly bade them goodbye before opening fire.

By now a throng was converging on the hotel, pouring into the backyard and clustering around to gawk at the battered corpse.

"What's happened?"

"Where's the sheriff?"

"This feller's a mess, an' shot besides!"

"Are there any more? Sounded like a war to me!"

Sheriff Ballard broke through the crowd, glanced at the body, and then faced Jessie. His stern face was mottled with perplexity.

"Get a posse together," she said urgently. "Quick!"

"Why for?"

"A gang of Renegaders just raided the hotel, killed the staff and a half-dozen guests. We got some of them"—Jessie nudged the body with the toe of her boot—"but not before they'd snatched Don Felipe De Baca, a special Mexican envoy and a very, *very* important man."

"Migawd, y'mean they made off with this feller?"

"Two of them did, while the rest held us at bay. There's another one high-tailing it after them. Hurry! There's still a chance that you can catch up—if not with De Baca, then with this other one, who'll know at least where De Baca's being taken."

Sheriff Ballard whirled into action, barking orders,

sending men scurrying, even as more townsfolk arrived to gather around and question. Suddenly, above the clamor rose a strident, raspy voice:

"Damn Renegaders, it's them again, what'd I tell you? Rustlin', lootin', now massacrin' right here in Mosquero! By all that's holy, we can't let them get away with it!" Gesturing and scowling, August Polhaus stood righteously indignant, his jacket pulled back and tucked against the butt of a Smith & Wesson .44, his cartridge belt and holster set low and tied down as though to emphasize that he was tough and meant business. "This's our land now, God-given and American-proud, and we must protect it! We must hunt the devils, till every last Mex is swept from our—"

"Shut up, August, stop electioneering!" Ballard growled loudly. "You're not on a campaign toot for governor, so cork it till then!"

"It needs to be said now!" Polhaus retorted. "Somebody has to cry out against this menace, this Mexican plot to take our territory!"

"If that isn't the stupidest thing I've heard in ages," Jessie snapped. "The man they took is Mexican, he's one of their own."

"A trick! He must be in on it. They're *all* in on it! Well, I for one won't be fooled, won't be lulled! I aim to give 'em what-for!"

"Fine, August. Grab your horse and join in the posse."

"Don't waste my time, Ballard. Me and my crew will handle this our way, the right way, the only way!" With that, Polhaus pivoted on his heel and stalked away, calling to his ranch hands to follow.

Jessie watched him, perturbed. "He's a danger, Sheriff."

"Oh, Polhaus'll storm around some, harassing the Mexicans living over here, who're already scared shi— *wit*less, as it is. He's done it before. But he's of a mind to run for territorial office, so he won't actually burn 'em out or string 'em up or suchlike."

"But others, believing him, are liable to."

"What can I do?" Ballard shook his head sadly. "I can't stop Polhaus from speechifyin', or beef-brained idiots from listenin'."

"You can get your dadratted posse a-moving," a man called impatiently. "At this rate, them lobos'll get clean to the border!"

"Awright, awright, hold your water . . ."

The sheriff returned to gathering his forces and bawling commands. Jessie wished him luck and, with Ki falling in alongside, left the hubbub in the yard and headed back to the Mirador. They were midway there when the posse galloped past, whoops and curses filling the night air as thickly as the dust fountaining behind them.

Entering the Mirador's lobby, they glimpsed the desk clerk sneaking a quick snort from a pint of whiskey. Spotting them, the clerk hastily stashed the bottle under the counter.

"Was just goin' off duty," the clerk explained sheepishly. "Hey, what was all that hoopla? I thought I heard shots."

"You did," Jessie said, and started up the stairs.

"Nothin' like that in here, thank God," the clerk called after them. "Nary a peep, quieter'n a prairie dog's burrow, it's been."

Not bothering to respond, Jessie and Ki reached the landing and strode down the hallway toward Harrigan's room. Flynn and McHugh barreled out from next door, revolvers drawn and cocked to fire.

"Easy," Ki cautioned.

"Didn't know it was you," Flynn said, holstering his piece.

"Yeah, whatever that ruckus was out there kinda put us on edge," McHugh added. "Sounded like it came from Old Town, where you went."

Jessica knocked on Harrigan's door. "It did. Some Renegaders attacked the inn there." She knocked again, but there was still no response. "The sheriff's out leading a posse to track them down."

"Hope he nails 'em. It's gotten awful ugly around here of a sudden," Flynn said, then scratched his head. "Huh. Mr. Harrigan seems to sure sleep soundly, don't he?"

"Not with his wound, he wouldn't," Ki replied, growing uneasy.

"Maybe it was that tetch of bourbon the doc sent up," McHugh suggested. "I recollect once when Wilmer downstairs drank his way through a gunfight. Woke up and swore he'd never heard a thing."

"Victor?" She tried the door, but it was locked. *"Victor!"*

She was answered only by silence.

McHugh said, "If you want, I'll get a key from the clerk."

Jessie stepped back a pace and said, "Break the door in."

Flynn looked at McHugh; McHugh nodded, and together they shouldered the door until its lockbolt split from the jamb. They lunged inside. The room

36

was dark, save for the pale light of a first-quarter moon seeping through the open window. The bed was rumpled, its covers thrown back, and it was empty.

"Where is he?" Flynn blurted. "He can't've gone!"

"Well, he's not here," Jessie retorted, staring about.

Ki lit the banquet lamp on the bureau, glancing at the tray of half-eaten food beside it, and then at Harrigan's gladstone bag. "His bag is still here, but this doesn't make any sense. He had no reason, and was in no condition to simply up and leave."

"He didn't," McHugh declared. "We'd have heard him."

"Did anyone visit him?" Jessica asked.

McHugh shook his head. "Only Wilmer with the tray."

"Appears the clerk shortchanged you, Jessie," Ki said with a thin, mirthless grin. "That was Harrigan's whiskey he was drinking."

"I bet you're right, Ki. There's no sign of a bottle here."

"No, a full pint was on the tray when Wilmer brought it up," Flynn said, then frowned and added stoutly, "Hey, now, we didn't swipe his whiskey. We've been sober and wide awake the whole time."

Jessie nodded. "I'm sure you were, and I'm sure you would've heard Mr. Harrigan if he'd tried to leave. I'm also sure he didn't. He couldn't have; his key's still in the lock, on this side of the door."

While they'd been talking, Ki had moved to peer out the window. Directly beneath the window was a narrow shade-roof that spanned the length of a plank-board alleyway running along the side of the building. Dropping from the window to the roof and then to the ground wouldn't have been overly difficult—except for a man with a bullet-crippled leg—but it would have been noisy enough to attract attention.

As Ki pulled his head back inside, a splinter in the sill pricked his hand. Checking it, he saw a couple of odd marks in the wood. He stepped back, regarding the window as a whole.

"Jessie, did you leave the sash all the way up?"

"No, I only cracked it a couple of inches. Why?"

He didn't answer, but looked out the window again, frowning in irritation. "I'm going down on the roof outside," he told the deputies. "I'll need a hand coming up again, okay?"

"Sure thing," McHugh said, plainly mystified.

Swinging his legs over the sill and downward along the siding, Ki dropped easily to the shade-roof. He crouched, examining the dust-coated boards, and after a few minutes he located scratches that were the same distance apart as the scrape marks on the window sill. Straightening, he hurried to the far end of the roof, studying its edges and surveying the night-shrouded rear of the hotel. Then he returned to the spot beneath the window, and was helped back into the room.

"Find anything?" Jessie asked.

"I think so," Ki replied tightly. He pointed out the two marks on the sill, and told of finding similar scrapings on the roof boards. "I think the gouges on the roof were made by the legs of a ladder, and the scratches here on the sill by hooks nailed to the ladder's top."

Flynn looked skeptical. "Where'd Mr. Harrigan get a ladder?"

"It wasn't *his* ladder," Jessie said grimly, catching Ki's drift. "He'd have a devil of a time climbing down one, even if he'd wanted to. But it would've been

38

relatively easy for some men to put up a ladder, sneak in, and haul Victor back down."

"They'd have to be powerful quiet about it, though I gotta admit we didn't have our window open, and there was all that gunfire 'n racket—" McHugh shook his head, still unconvinced. "Even if we missed hearing them, Mr. Harrigan surely would've. He'd have woken and hollered, long afore they could've reached his bed an' gagged him, or clunked him noddy with a gun butt or whatever."

"Not if he'd been drugged first," Jessica replied.

"Drugged? But how?"

"The whiskey."

"Not bad, Jessie, not bad at all," Ki allowed. "That'd also explain where the bottle went; they took it to remove the evidence."

McHugh's eyes narrowed. "Reckon we oughta visit Wilmer."

The four left the room, Flynn closing the door behind them. Reaching the lobby, they saw that Wilmer was gone; a different clerk, beanpole-tall and bespectacled, now stood behind the counter.

The clerk smiled ingratiatingly. "Good evenin'."

"What're you doing here, Godwin?" McHugh barked.

"W-why, working," the clerk stammered, taken aback.

"Damn," Ki swore. "Wilmer did say he was going off duty."

Flynn, impetuous with anger, leaned across the counter and grasped the clerk by his shirtfront. "Where'd Wilmer go, Godwin?"

"I dunno! Out drinking? Or maybe home? How should I know?"

"There're a score of saloons, and he likes 'em all," Flynn growled, thrusting the clerk away. "We'd best try his home first."

"You know where he lives?" Jessie asked.

"Sure, in a shanty out behind the freighter's," McHugh answered, and nodded to the clerk. "Thanks, Godwin. Much obliged."

Face flushed and glasses askew, the clerk bawled, "I'll report you for this!" as the four turned and hastened outside.

With McHugh leading, they strode hastily along the boardwalk, then angled across toward a large, nondescript barn set back from the main street. Over the barn's double-doored entrance was a sign: TRANSPORT & STORAGE, T. T. PHONLEY, PROP. The doors were padlocked, the adjoining wagon yard was deserted, and the weedy lot on the barn's other side was empty, as far as could be seen.

They headed across the lot, which extended out and around the rear of the barn. It was a dump of old empty barrels and crates, broken wagon parts, and similar refuse. In the midst of the litter, looking much a part of it, loomed a dilapidated cabin, tarpaper-roofed and sunbleached, tilting on a rotted foundation. Lamplight glowed through the worn shade of the cracked front window, and a saddled horse stood with trailing reins near the front door.

"Nice horse for a clerk," Jessie noted as they approached.

"Can't be Wilmer's," McHugh said. "He can't afford crowbait—"

A scream cut him off. It was high and piercing, yet it was unmistakably the cry of a man. Ki plunged for the shack, the deputies a pace behind and drawing their pistols, while the scream faded to a whimpering gurgle. Not bothering to learn whether it was locked or not, they hit the door in a flying wedge that almost twisted its hinges off.

The interior was a decrepit hovel, stinking of liquor and sweat. Wilmer was doubled over in a stoop, moaning piteously, one hand grasping a chair back for support, the other pressing against his belly. A thick-bodied, bristle-bearded man was swiveling from Wilmer to face the door, a skinning knife in hand, blood smearing its slender blade.

They rushed at the man, who reacted with speed and dexterity, dodging aside, reversing the knife to toss it, while cross-drawing a vintage Remington .44.

Ki launched into a *tobi-geri*, a flying snap-kick, aiming to strike the man's solar plexus hard enough to incapacitate but not to kill. Simultaneous with his spring, the knife flashed by to bury itself in the door-jamb, and Flynn impulsively shot the man in the chest. The man lurched askew from the slug's impact, and Ki slammed into him off-center, clipping his ribs. The man reeled away, slack-jawed, falling in a spiraling crumple as his legs gave beneath him. He landed face-up, the final pumpings of his heart spurting crimson across his chest.

"What kinda fool stunt was that, bouncin' at him unarmed an' all!" Flynn snapped at Ki. "I come near to pluggin' you instead!"

"Dead men can't talk," Ki said, and turned, exasperated, to where Jessie was now kneeling beside the hotel clerk.

She glanced up. "Well, Wilmer's still alive. Barely."

The clerk had slumped to a crouch and was on the

verge of keeling over. Blood was riveting between the fingers clutching his belly as he moaned feebly, fearfully, knowing a gut wound could mean hours, even days, of remorseless agony before eventual death.

"I'll get the doc," McHugh said. "If I can find him."

"Try La Posada Duquesa," Jessica suggested.

McHugh nodded, trotting out the door. Then Ki and Flynn carried Wilmer over to the grubby folding cot the clerk used as a bed. His anguished whimpers trailed off into raspy breathing, and he lapsed into unconsciousness as they stretched him out and loosened his clothing. His skin was pallid and moist, and he was having trouble breathing, so Jessie wadded the single threadbare blanket under his head and shoulders, and crouched, keeping watch.

Ten minutes later, McHugh returned with Doc Scofield.

"Understand you got a live one," Scofield said by way of greeting. "That'll be refreshing, after the batch at the inn."

Jessie sighed, leading him to Wilmer. "You may be unable to save this one either, Doctor, but we need him alive and conscious enough to talk. You think you can bring him around?"

"I'll do m'best, but I ain't guaranteein' . . ."

While Scofield labored over Wilmer, Jessie lit a fire in the shack's rusty potbellied stove, to boil water and cleanse dressings. Flynn went outside to scavenge slats from the crates to use as firewood. Ki and McHugh grouped around the body of the dead man, McHugh fishing through the pockets for something that might identify him.

"Nothing," McHugh said disgustedly when he was

42

finished. He surveyed the meager pile—a pencil stub, cigarette papers, and a sack of Bull Durham, a token to a whorehouse in Nogales, and a drawstring poke containing twenty silver dollars—and he added, "Nothing but a stranger with twenty pieces of silver, his payment to kill Wilmer."

Ki nodded. "Let's hope he doesn't earn his blood money."

An hour passed before the doctor was through. "Reckon he'll make it. Doesn't seem any vital organ got hit, and that's the trick. But he's terribly weak, and infection could set in later."

"Can he talk?" Flynn asked.

"He can, when he becomes conscious." Scofield repacked his satchel and started for the door. "Whether he *will* is another matter."

Flynn swore with impatience. Yet there was nothing any of them could do until Wilmer came to of his own accord. Another hour dragged by. Finally McHugh, almost as frustrated as his restless partner, stretched and declared, "Hell, this ain't doing nobody no good, and I've still got a town to patrol. I think I'll go make my tour around."

"Don't forget to mosey back," Flynn groused, then said to Jessie, "You might as well take a breather, too. If you ain't et yet, stop in at Digbert's, across the street from the hotel."

Jessica and Ki decided to do just that, not having had a meal since box-lunching on the train. They first returned to the Mirador, where they changed clothes— Jessie to worn, tight-fitting jeans, a clean man's-style blouse, and a denim jacket; and Ki to Levi's, a collarless shirt, and comfortable rope-soled slippers in place of his dressier, ankle-high boots. And both made certain to rearm themselves before leaving—Jessie with her .38 snugged in a holster and a two-shot derringer secreted behind the wide buckle of her belt; and Ki with his arsenal of small weaponry now stashed in the many pockets and loops of a scuffed, loose-draping black leather vest.

The cuisine at Digbert's proved to be a good-news/bad-news proposition, the bad news being that it was terrible, the good news being that there was plenty of it. They ate quickly and went back to the cabin.

Wilmer's condition was unchanged. They waited some more. McHugh showed up and, with Ki and Flynn, hauled the dead man outside, covering him with a crate so that animals couldn't get to him before the undertaker could in the morning. McHugh then stuck around, while Flynn took a well-earned break. Jessie began pacing the cabin. Ki settled into a cross-legged, cross-armed position—one that he used for relaxation and to renew the life-energy that was the basis of martial-arts philosophy—but even he had trouble calming his thwarted urge for action.

Flynn arrived, and McHugh, using his excuse of being the deputy on night duty, went on another of his tours. Shortly after he left, Wilmer awoke with a tormented whine. The remaining three grouped around his cot, studying the twitching, frightened clerk.

"L-leave me alone . . . No, don't . . . don't . . ."

"Snap out of it," Flynn said. "We won't hurt you."

Wilmer's eyelids fluttered. "Wh-wha . . . ? You . . . ?"

"Who knifed you, Wilmer? Why'd he do it?"

"No! Don't let him!"

"He's dead," Jessie said soothingly. "Why'd he knife you?"

"I dunno, I . . . 'Posed to pay me, not kill me . . ."

44

Wilmer hesitated, as if realizing he was talking himself into prison.

"If you don't help us, we can't help you," Ki said shrewdly.

Wilmer swallowed thickly, his watery eyes glazed with pain and fear. Perhaps from a desire for protection, or a hunger for revenge, or simply because the attempt on his life had robbed him of resistance, he nodded weakly after a moment and confessed. "I was to get ten dollars from him, for doping Mr. Harrigan's whiskey with laudanum. A whole ten bucks, just for that and keeping m' mouth shut. Hell, easy money."

"Not this time," Jessica said. "Who wanted it done?"

"The gent who hired me, Enoch Yates."

Flynn reared back, startled. "The mine owner?"

Wilmer nodded again, coughed, but kept on feebly, "Some mine... 'S all played out, never was much... Didn't think of it when Yates first came to me, but I see it now. Sour Mule Valley's nothin' but wilds, an' his mine would be perfect to hide somebody..."

"Did Yates tell you he wanted to take Harrigan, or why?"

"No... Didn't have no idea of it when he hired me. When it happened, it was too late for me to do anything, y'see that, don't you? So I waited here for my money, like I was supposed to, only instead of Yates paying me, this gent I never seed before stabbed me..."

A fever seemed to be burning in Wilmer's sick eyes, and he struggled to rise, his fingers clawing at Jessie. "You gotta believe me, I didn't know they were gonna grab your friend, and I still don't know why they wanted him. Honest, you gotta believe me!"

45

"Rest," Jessie said gently, easing him down. "You must save your strength. Doc Scofield will look in on you later, but rest for now."

"You . . . you can't go!"

"Sorry, but we have to."

"But that hombre . . . his friends . . . they might . . ."

"Your pal ain't goin' to bother nothin' but the worms," Flynn declared, frowning down at the clerk. "Only worry you got is us gettin' Mr. Harrigan back in one piece. Cooperatin' like this'll make it go easier on you, but you still could be a partner to murder."

Wilmer sank lower in his cot and began to weep softly.

Jessie, Ki, and the deputy had no more time to spend on him. Enough time had been wasted already, and further delays were inevitable. McHugh had to be informed, although, as night deputy, he'd have to stay in town for Sheriff Ballard's return. The hostler had to be rousted, so that Jessie and Ki could rent horses and gear. Flynn tried to argue them out of it, but since everyone else who'd join a posse was already in one, they were the only ones left to side him. Besides, they were adamant, and there wasn't time to debate it.

That was the trouble. Time was as much their enemy now as were the kidnappers.

★

Chapter 4

The three riders topped out on a ridge above Sour Mule Valley and reined in. It was nearly midnight now, and the pale quarter-moon and sprinkling of stars cast meager light. Darkness blurred the rugged harshness of the surrounding terrain; the valley itself was swathed in gloom, falling steeply away from the ridge in black, corrugated smudges of boulders and sparse desert growth.

"Down there?" Jessie asked, gesturing at the narrow trail that wound through obscured cholla thickets and clumps of tall mescal.

Flynn nodded, stretching his weary muscles in the saddle. "Yates's claim would be 'tween here and the valley floor, along with the few others that were staked. Here in Sour Mule was the only place anywhere close to Mosquero that silver was found."

"Nope. Never had much reason to come out before, and Yates was always just another Valley miner to me. There're a number of 'em, stakin' and swappin'. Their digs seem to change hands faster 'n partners at a square dance." The deputy rubbed his jaw. "I figure Yates can't be usin' a small one for this job, and the couple of big digs I know are nearby. We just keep to the path, we'll come to 'em. They've both been deserted for some time."

"Let's take it slowly," Ki cautioned. "There's no

47

telling what Yates'll do to Harrigan if we give him advance warning."

"Yeah, sneaky does it." Flynn edged his horse forward, Jessie and Ki following on their livery rentals. Carefully they studied the path and sides for signs of recent activity, but were unable to find any clues until Ki, riding point, spied a cigar butt.

They dismounted and scouted the immediate area. Jessie located some hoofprints leading off the trail, and Flynn confirmed that the direction of the tracks led to one of the two large mines.

Deciding to approach the mine cross-country, rather than by tracing the prints, they quietly eased their horses down across the hillside, keeping out of sight as much as possible. They blazed their own trail, weaving through the indistinct scrub and rock, clawing along steep slopes and declivities where their horses almost slid on their hindquarters.

"We dasn't go much farther on horseback," Flynn said at last. "Too dangerous, and too noisy once we get close to the mine."

Agreeing, Jessie and Ki swung out of their saddles. Single file, they led their mounts as they continued breaking path across the desolate valley, forging through brush and between boulders, occasionally sinking leg-deep in slides of soft shale. For a quarter-mile they wound in and out, making a wide, vague loop to avoid both the hoofprint path and the regular trail. They figured that if the mine ahead was where Yates had taken Harrigan, then the man would likely have posted guards there to watch their backpath and the trail. Their only chance to catch Yates unawares was to attack from an unexpected direction—and even that chance was an iffy proposition.

Eventually they came upon a huge gap where, centuries before, a boulder had dislodged and crashed down into the valley, leaving a sheer but natural pocket. Anchoring their horses' reins with rocks, they crawled up to the rim of the pocket.

"The mine," Flynn whispered, peering over.

Joining him at the edge, Jessie and Ki saw that in front of them a gravelly hillside sloped gradually for some twenty-five or thirty feet to a rubble-strewn basin. In the slope directly opposite them was a narrow gap—obviously the main entrance to the basin—and not far from it were the sides and roof of a shaft house, around which were heaped mine tailings and discarded equipment.

Jessica murmured, "Yes, but is this—"

"It is," Ki confirmed, sounding none too thrilled about it. A moment before, he'd glimpsed a brief flash among the rocks at the bottom of the hillside—a spark no brighter or longer than a firefly's wink—or a match's flare when lighting a cigar. Focusing intently, he perceived two vague outlines; they were a deeper black than the diffused darkness of night, but could have been mistaken for boulders, if they hadn't shifted restlessly.

"Two men are sitting right below us," Ki said, pointing them out. "This is the place, all right. They wouldn't be here otherwise."

"Strange, though, them being *here* instead of at the shaft house."

"Smart, Jessie. By stationing themselves across the basin and facing the shaft house, they not only act as guards, but can catch anyone entering the basin in a crossfire. It won't be easy to creep up on them."

"Then we'll just have to rush 'em," Flynn said, rising.

"Wait—"

Flynn didn't wait. With the same impulsiveness he'd shown before, the deputy scrambled over the rim, gripping an old .50-caliber Spencer repeater he'd taken from his saddle scabbard. He plummeted down the slope, risking a tumble in his haste, but impetuously convinced that this was how best to drop the guards—short of shooting them outright, which could very well alert the rest of the gang.

Jessie and Ki leaped after him, quickly if apprehensively.

They were almost as startled as the guards, when Flynn's rash assault actually worked. "Freeze, you varmints!" Flynn roared, leveling his carbine, catching the pair before they could turn and bring their rifles to bear. Wisely they froze, except for their hands slowly rising above their heads, the faces clearly astonished.

Jessie and Ki moved in to disarm them, staying wide of Flynn's carbine in case there was a tussle. There was one, and it came suddenly, but not from the men Flynn was covering.

In through the gap came a body of armed riders. One glance told Jessie and Ki this was no posse of townsfolk; the riders charged ahead, opening fire.

Desperately they all sprang for cover, lashed by a hail of bullets. Shooting from horseback made for lousy accuracy, which was their only salvation as they dove behind boulders. The two guards, weaponless, scuttled higher along the hillside in a frenzied attempt to escape. Flynn dug in and began returning fire with his carbine; while Jessica, dodging behind an outcrop with both guards' rifles, started triggering and levering as fast as she could. And Ki realized bleakly that if Harrigan was ever to be rescued, it would have to be now.

"Cover me!" he shouted, and launched into a zig-zagging sprint around the rock-strewn perimeter of the basin.

Jessie and Flynn responded with an increased barrage. Yet there were just two against many, and some of the many kept concentrating on Ki. Lead spanged and ricocheted about him, a vortex of rock shards and fragmented grit stinging his flesh as he ran, hunching low, darting from boulder to boulder. If and when he reached the shaft house—where, most logically, Harrigan was hidden—he'd be fairly well protected from gunfire. Ahead, however, between him and the shaft house, loomed a mounded hillock of tailings, fill, and loose shale, stretching like a barren plateau that offered him no concealment other than the dubious shroud of night.

The riders were dismounting now and scattering for cover, leaving three dead and a fourth wounded on the basin floor. Only Jessie and Flynn's determined firing held them down. In a one-two punch, Jessie winged a bearded man in the shoulder, while Flynn blew the face off another . . . and Ki dove up the mound.

He sank at his first step. Pulling free, he struggled higher, trying not to slide back, clawing, almost swimming, the incline sucking him in and down as treacherously as quicksand. He found a few solid places, but every inch was a fight, a slow, enervating battle that left him exposed to the mercy of the gunmen.

Bullets whined close, or drilled deep in around him. One man rose to take a careful bead; an instant before he triggered, Jessie fired, her slug glancing off the man's belt buckle and tearing up through his belly. His carbine empty, Flynn drew his plow-handled .45, then staggered, feeling a quick burning cut across his scalp. Blood flowed down from the furrowed wound,

51

but he disregarded it, blasting two shots at a thin man scurrying for a better vantage. The man buck-jumped, sprawling grotesquely, holding his shattered leg.

Ki continued his gradual worming up the loose-packed mound, expecting to be shot with every torturous step he took. Eventually he gained the top and flung himself, rolling, away from sight. The crest of the mound was bare and narrow, and it extended all the way to the shaft house. Cautiously he approached, hugging the mound, until he got to the corner of the shaft house and slid behind it.

Harrigan was not in the shaft house. Nobody was in the shaft house, Ki saw, for the rear and far side of the structure had caved in, exposing collapsed supports and the mouth of the mine tunnel.

Gently he slipped down from the mound. No gunfire had been coming from the shaft house, and no sign of men could be seen now, yet Ki remained wary, his senses straining to catch the slightest noise or motion. Edging inside the shaft house and working his way through the maze of crumbled timbers, he dropped to the mine tunnel and crouched silently in the debris by its entrance.

No sound echoed from within. Ki picked up a stone and chucked it inside. The stone hit a wall, the hollow clunk of its impact fading away. Ki waited a minute longer, then eased slowly into the tunnel.

After some yards the tunnel curved abruptly, the result of the original miners following a particular seam of ore. Ki groped around the corner, went on like a blind man for another short distance, then made two more turns and found that the rest of the passage was lit by mesquite torches. They were stuck in wall niches at infrequent intervals, the mesquite providing very poor light, but at least now Ki could see well enough to avoid the clogging earthslides and fallen beams.

He moved forward as quietly as he could, picking his way over the solid floor as though it were more loose shale. There was an icy clamminess in the saddle of his back, for Ki had the distinct sensation that he was not alone. He hoped his intuitive feeling was because he was closing in on Victor Harrigan, but another part of his brain kept warning him that if Harrigan was in here, so Yates would be.

Creeping along through the dim, smoky murk, he saw that ahead the tunnel widened into a grottolike cavern, with still more mesquite torches ringing the small chamber. He glided closer, his rope-soled slippers padding as softly as moccasins...a step farther...and he glimpsed a length of rope curled haphazardly in one corner, along with the flannel nightshirt Harrigan had been wearing in bed. Crossing swiftly, he hunkered and began checking the nightshirt for possible clues.

"Hold it," a voice snarled.

Ki whirled, his hand dipping to his vest, but there was nobody else in the cavern. Stymied, he straightened and let his hand fall.

A nasty chuckle came from where the tunnel continued on the other side of the cavern. "Good boy. I gotcha smack in m'sights."

Out of the black maw of the tunnel stepped a short, swarthy man with salt-and-pepper hair thick at the temples but sparse on the crown. He was grinning, showing rotted teeth in gray gums; and he was training a ten-gauge Ithaca double-barreled shotgun directly at Ki's chest.

"Enoch Yates," Ki stated.

"Uh-huh. And you'd be the slant-eyes pallin' with Harrigan."

"Where is he?"

"Never mind. Where's that pretty lady?"

"In Mosquero."

Yates shrugged. "Eh, it'd have been nice to send you both as a bonus, but I guess one of you'll do. Now drop your gun."

"I'm not carrying one," Ki replied, and made a slow circle, hands upraised, to prove his point. "You sending me to Harrigan?"

"You're mighty curious to know where he's got to, ain'tcha?" Yates's grin broadened. "He's gone. On his way, like we'll be."

Hearing the faint, sporadic gunfire reverberating from outside the mine, Ki asked, "What about De Baca?"

"I dunno no De Baca, don't care to know, neither." Sobering, Yates motioned with his shotgun. "Enough palaver. It's time we was pullin' out, less'n you'd like to stay here permanent-like."

"You'll never get past the posse in the basin."

"No?" Yates spat contemptuously, and for a moment Ki thought he'd caught on to his lie. Then Yates said, "The tunnel behind me bores clear through to the other side of the butte. Before anyone out front figures it out, our trail will be too cold to follow."

"To where? The Portrillos?"

"Boy, there you go again, gettin' uppity with your sniffer." Yates gestured again with the shotgun. "You'll find out soon enough."

Ki's lips tightened in a thin, metallic smile as he moved toward the tunnel. Right now Yates held the high card, the shotgun; there wasn't enough room to elude its pattern of buck. He'd have to bide his time and wait for an opening that might never occur.

"Take a torch," Yates ordered. Ki wrenched one of the torches from its niche, and as he did so, he noticed that the gunfire in the basin had ceased. Yates noticed the silence too. "Hurry," he snapped. "I'll be on your ass, and I can't miss it."

Ki entered the tunnel, which was smaller and in worse condition than the one leading in from the shaft house. It was less than five feet high and choked with slides and timbers, forcing them to walk hunched over, often squeezing through the rubble. Darkness fell away before the advancing torchlight, Yates's footsteps resounding off the shored rock walls. The tunnel unraveled in gentle curves and dips, like an endlessly long and very lazy snake, but finally they exited through a tapering, partially obstructed crevice, onto a ridge overlooking the deep gorge of a prehistoric riverbed.

"Go on," Yates prompted. "Go on, boy, to your left."

Turning, Ki started along the ridge. The narrow path threaded into dim obscurity in both directions, skirting the gorge on one side, and hemmed in by clumped boulders on the other. Ki didn't like it, not at all, but at least here he was alone with Yates. He didn't know how long that would hold true; there could easily be another pack of riders ahead, waiting to accompany Yates on his getaway. Anything like that would spoil all his chances of forcing Yates to talk.

When Ki came to a slightly wider patch, he purposely stumbled and hesitated, as though confused. Yates closed in and prodded him with the shotgun, barking, "C'mon, squinty, we're almost there."

Blinking, Ki looked about. "Where?"

"There! The horses!" Yates bellowed, thrusting the shotgun forward to indicate direction. And Ki, arching his spine so that the thrusting shotgun slid from the small of his back, pivoted with his left arm, deflecting the barrels away, his right hand stuffing the mesquite torch into Yates's face.

Yates howled shrilly as flames seared his eyes, his hair, the flesh of his nose and cheeks. He pawed with his free hand, while reflexively he triggered one of the barrels. The erupting discharge was so close to Ki that he could feel the heat of the muzzle blast, the shockwave from spewing buckshot—but by then he'd tossed the torch aside and was sweeping his right hand in a paralyzing, stiff-fingered jab to Yates's midriff, while circling his left up and around in a slashing chop to the miner's gun wrist.

The shotgun dropped from Yates's nerveless fingers. Eyebrows and hair singed, skin reddened from the fire, Yates gagged, retching from Ki's blow to his belly. He staggered back, mindless with pain, his foot slipping on the edge of the path. He wavered—

Ki grabbed Yates and swung him in from the crumbling brink. Stooping slightly, Yates teetered toward Ki as though blinded—but it was a trick, to disguise his drawing of a concealed four-barrel .32 Sharps "stingy gun." Straightening, he fired at Ki.

Ki ducked one way and jerked Yates roughly the other, as the small, derringer-type hideout pistol detonated, its bullet virtually parting Ki's hair. Cursing himself for having tempered the force of his spearhead jab—and yet knowing he had to hold back, if Yates was to be in condition to talk—Ki delivered an elbow smash to the same, now very tender spot in Yates's midriff.

Yates doubled over again, this time genuinely, frogging backward from the momentum of Ki's blow. The shale beneath his boots disintegrated into gravel, and he swayed off balance.

Ki already had a grip on Yates, his left hand having clamped around the stingy gun to wrest it away while preventing Yates from recocking it. Yates, insane with panic and agony, kept struggling to wrench loose. Ki was reaching to get a second, firmer hold on Yates with his right hand, when suddenly the frantic miner tugged free, inexplicably letting go of his gun and twisting around as though to escape. Ki was left clasping the stingy gun, while Yates walked in a headlong plunge over the enbankment.

A soulful wail of horror echoed up, receding hollowly with the miner into the gorge's black depths. There was a soft, distant thump of meat striking rock, and then silence.

Ki leaned against a boulder, catching his breath. Then, in a rare fit of temper and frustration, he went to the brink and yelled down, "Goddamn you, Yates, what did you do that for? I wanted you alive!" Snatching up the torch, he relit it and stalked toward the mine-shaft entrance, not feeling one whit salved by his outburst. . . .

Arriving back at the basin, however, Ki was relieved to find that Jessie and Flynn had survived the fray. The deputy had knotted his kerchief around his bullet-furrowed scalp, and was hobbling about, searching for a boot heel that had been shot off. Jessie was tending the few wounded gunmen, the rest of the bunch having either died or fled. Mostly they'd fled,

57

being hardly more than border scum working from order to order, poorly paid and utterly disinclined to battle stubbornly over something they knew nothing about.

So they were of little help. Of even less value were Harrigan's discarded nightshirt, the rope that had apparently been used to bind him when he'd been abducted, and Yates's meager belongings, which were also found stashed in the tunnel. While Flynn remained to watch the gunmen, Jessie and Ki scouted the basin and mine entrances for signs of Harrigan's departure; they located the horses Yates had been attempting to reach, but what with the night, all the comings and goings, and the stony barrenness of Sour Mule Valley, picking out and following a specific set of tracks proved to be fruitless.

Bone-weary and depressed, they returned to Mosquero.

In town, they learned that Sheriff Ballard was still out with his posse. Flynn and McHugh jailed the gunnies they'd brought back from the basin, then went to wake Doc Scofield with the news of more business. The news spread as well through the saloons and gambling parlors, unsettling the town further, adding to the aura of fear and rage.

"Thank heavens Polhaus isn't here to enflame passions more," Jessie told Ki as they headed to their hotel. "The area's whipped almost to a fever pitch, and once it blows, it'll never stop."

Behind the lobby counter, the clerk was tilted back in a chair, snoring gustily. Jessie and Ki collected their keys without disturbing his sleep, and went upstairs to their rooms.

• • •

Jessica Starbuck sat on the edge of the bed and, sighing, pulled off her boots. The floor was cold to her feet as she padded over to lower the window blind and draw the curtains. She then stripped naked, filled the chipped washbowl with water from the matching pitcher, and used a hand towel to scrub herself.

She would have adored a hot bath and a chance to wash her hair, but that, like so many other things now, would have to wait until morning. Constantly rinsing out the towel, she made do by sluicing off a good portion of Sour Mule Valley that was clinging like a patina to her face, limbs, breasts, and loins. Briskly she dried herself with the larger, if equally threadbare bath towel. Her nude flesh tingled, her skin glowing a healthy pink, as she slipped on the chemise nightgown she took from her bellows case. Then, after brushing out her hair and pinning it up, she doused the lamp and climbed into bed.

And lay there, thinking.

De Baca was missing, Harrigan was missing, and in less than two days, the train for the conference would be arriving. Something had to be done, and damned fast, yet their choices were limited, as far as she could see. Probably the best odds lay in returning to the mine, where, during daylight, a concerted effort could be made to trace Harrigan's direction. And at that, she thought dejectedly, the odds were slim. What a mess. Sometimes things worked out simply, and other times they didn't; this was turning out to be one of those times when things didn't, with a vengence.

On that note, Jessie, exhausted, fell into a deep slumber. . . .

• • •

Ki, too, had decided on a quick cat-bath before re-
tiring. He peeled off his soiled, sweat-soggy clothes
and proceeded to wash away the grime. He was working with the towel when he heard someone stop out
in the hall, and knuckles tapped softly on his door.

"Hello? Are you awake?"

It was a girl's voice, shy and anxious, but Ki didn't
answer. He'd had enough of voice-luring traps for one
day, and he was none too keen about this hotel, either.
Instinctively his eyes checked the door and window;
the lock was engaged and the blind fully drawn.

"Hello?" the voice repeated. "I'm Evita De Baca."

Ki padded barefoot to the door and pressed his ear
to its panel. He didn't catch anything suspicious, no
heavy creaking of boots, no low breathing of men
waiting with her. He whispered, "Who, Señora?"

"Señorita. Señorita Evita De Baca, Felipe De Baca's daughter."

"What do you want, Señorita?"

"You must help me, you're my only hope!"

Ki thought that sounded a tad thick, but the name
of De Baca was not one he could easily ignore. "Don't
come in until I tell you to."

"Very well . . . but hurry!"

Ki unlatched the door and went back to his clothes,
slipping on his jeans for modesty and his vest for
precaution. Then he called out, and the door opened
just enough to allow a petite young woman with Latin
features to ease inside. She shut it behind her at once.

"Lock it," Ki said, and while she did, he scratched
his bare chest and added, "I wasn't expecting visitors,
especially a lady."

"A lady in this country grows up seeing men in all

60

states of undress," she replied demurely, starting toward him. "It is I who should be thought improper, coming here alone and at this hour."

"That's far enough."

She stopped, puzzled.

The girl was twenty-two, maybe twenty-three, certainly no older. She had an oval face with a snub nose, a full mouth that was almost too wide, and brooding eyes that were dark and moist, like olives. Her black, tangled hair was shot with sunbleached tendrils. She wore slim leather huaraches, and a thin pink *camisa* that did little to disguise a lean-hipped, pert-breasted figure that intimated a sly sensuality. She didn't appear to be concealing any weapons—but neither did Ki, and, knowledge making him wary, he wished to keep a distance.

He said, "Why would De Baca's daughter be in Mosquero?"

"Father sent for me, didn't you know?"

Ki shook his head. "I didn't even know he had children."

"Seven, and one on the way. But we haven't seen each other in many months," Evita explained, and forgetting Ki's warning, she came a step nearer. "So when Father was appointed emissary, he—"

"No closer. I mean it."

Again she hesitated, looking perplexed. She glanced down, smoothing her palms along her *camisa*, and then comprehension dawned in her eyes. "Ahh! You suspect I hide something dangerous. Well . . ."

Ki thought himself prepared for any move, but he was taken by surprise when Evita abruptly crossed her arms and began lifting her *camisa*.

"Father cabled me to meet him," she continued,

blithely revealing slender legs and the boyish curve of her thighs. "I've been attending college in Santa Fe, you see, studying English literature."

"I'm seeing more than that! You don't have—"

"You made your objection quite plain." Her tone held a subtle mockery. She brushed the *camisa* off and let it drop to the floor, and stood, hands on hips, exposing smooth, unblemished skin, pointed breasts topped by raspberry-sized nipples, and a pair of skimpy muslin drawers. "Satisfied? Or do you want *mis calzones* off, too?"

"Don't tempt me," Ki said slowly.

"He threatens," she scoffed. "So brave, so masterful!"

"Listen, Evita, I was only being careful."

"Yes, yes I understand." Her eyes grew troubled again, and her hands fell to her sides in nervous fists. "It is why I sought you out, having heard of your courage when my father was kidnapped." She advanced, her voice shaky, and this time Ki did not object. "When I arrived a short while ago, and learned of the Renegaders..."

Ki stirred uneasily, conscious of her lithe, near-naked femininity as she moved closer. "I...I'm sorry about your father, but there's every reason to believe he's still alive."

"Save him," she pleaded, laying her hand on his arm. Her fingers quivered and she gripped tighter. "You must save him."

"If there's a way, we'll do it."

"Yes, you are a strong one," she murmured, scrutinizing him with her dark, luminous eyes. Her chin was raised, and her uptilted face was yearning. "Your caution comes from judgment, from staking your life and winning. You do not fear me. Perhaps you fear *for* me."

Ki was growing aroused, but he was also growing tired of her ploy. He wondered how far he could get with her, or rather, how far she'd go for what she wanted of him. She was now so close he could smell her lavender-scented soap, feel the warmth radiating from her... but eager as she might be, she evidently wanted him to make any initial pass. So Ki cupped her raised chin and kissed her.

She responded with enthusiasm, pressing her body against him, her arm circling his back and clinging for a long, burning moment.

Her fingers loosened, but she continued to press intimately, stretching on tiptoe. "You will help?" she coaxed, her hand creeping up along his back to his neck. "I'd be grateful, very grateful."

Ki smiled. "Would you, now?"

"I'd pay any price, make any sacrifice..."

Ki found himself being edged back toward the bed. "Why, Señorita De Baca, I'd hate to think you're trying to turn my head."

"I could never hope to trick a strong one like you," she sighed, leading him but allowing him to lead.

He drew her to him and then down onto the bed. She didn't resist. They kissed again, and Ki could feel his erection growing inside his jeans. Evita pushed her small hand up under his vest to caress his bare chest, touching his tiny nipples, the fringe of hair around each, the ripples of muscle on his ribs.

The kiss continued. They stretched out on the bed, her mouth glued to his, eyes closed, nostrils flaring. Her curious fingers found the bulge at his groin and traveled its length. She made a whimpering sound in

63

her throat, still not breaking the kiss. Ki held her gently, sensing that she was wet with anticipation as she traced the covered column of his thickening flesh.

Then her hand slid to his waistband. His rope belt was already undone, and she had no trouble popping the top button. She lifted her mouth from his and twisted around, her eyes heavy-lidded and sparkling while she unbuttoned his fly, tugging his jeans down. He arched his hips, and she used both hands to grasp his erection. "Ahhh, *es estupendo . . .*" She licked her lips.

Ki rubbed a hand over her buttocks. "Your drawers . . ."

"In a minute." She bent over him. As her head lowered, her eyes closed and her full-lipped mouth opened, her pink tongue fluting out to lick his shaft. She seemed to taste him, to see if she liked it, then she fitted her mouth over the silky crown.

Ki gasped and watched, his eyes flaring when her tongue went into action. His hips began to move slowly, but she stopped and lifted her head. She smiled. Sitting up on her heels, she untied the drawstring and eased her drawers down. "You too," she said, sliding them free. Her pudenda was plump, the lips accented by a thin line of velvety curls.

Ki slid out of his vest, and took five seconds to push his jeans the rest of the way down his legs, and off. Evita crawled lengthwise alongside him, and they kissed again, their mouths joining moistly together. Ki's hand dropped into the hollow of her loins, his fingers exploring the lightly haired pad of her mound, then moving lower, inside the lips of her cleft, one finger dipping easily into tight, slippery heat. She moaned in the kiss, her inner muscles working in a rhythmic, squeezing pulse around his finger.

"Ahora, ahora mismo," she mewed. "Now, right now..."

Ki nodded, his face taut with desire. He moved over her as her thighs splayed wide, her crotch glistening wetly. He pressed slowly, gently, and felt her stretching to accept him. He slid deeply into her, against increasing internal resistance. Her slim body trembled. She breathed quickly through her mouth. *"Más, más...* More, more..."

Ki glanced down at their merging loins in the dim lamplight, surprised that she was managing to take him all in. She was so small and slender, yet she was enveloping his entire length and girth. Her breathing was ragged, openmouthed, her eyes fluttering as his pubic bone nudged against her mound, his erection sunk in her to its hilt.

Ki lowered his head and their mouths touched, their tongues flicking in play. He withdrew slowly, his shaft moist with her secretions, then plunged back inside, then again and again, his tempo quickening. Evita shuddered and moaned, and her kiss became frantic.

Ki began a steady pumping into her tight, hot depths. She broke their kiss, gasping, whining, moving her hips in concert now, clenching her inner muscles. Ki could feel her mouth nibbling his ears, his cheek, while her pantings and groans became a continuous, low-pitched keening. *"Venga rápido*—come quickly. *Venga! Venga!"*

Her thighs pressed against Ki's legs, her ankles snaking over and locking around his calves as Ki plunged into her. He could feel himself growing and expanding till he felt as if he were going to explode from the exquisite pleasure building in him, and he could tell that Evita was nearing completion as she gripped him in the vise of her legs and worked more urgently beneath him.

Her Spanish pleadings choked off in a staccato sputtering as she pushed her belly up at him, shuddering convulsively in orgasm. Ki slowed his grinding thrusts, trying to savor the last delights. And then his mouth opened wide and he could no longer control, only yield, and he erupted inside her. He collapsed limply, and she lay still, pressed firmly around him.

When at last Ki rolled from her, they lay quietly side by side, exhausted, satiated. Finally, Evita yawned and rose from the bed.

"A towel," she explained sheepishly, stepping to the bureau. "I think you must have saved up for a year. Would you like a backrub?"

Ki nodded, smiling, and rolled over on his stomach, cradling his face in the pillow. He failed to see that along with the towel, Evita swept up the water pitcher. He failed to see her contented expression change to one of regretful determination, and her two swift, silent strides back to the bed, the pitcher high over her head.

All Ki knew was an abrupt, blinding explosion inside his brain, as the hard ceramic water pitcher collided with his skull. Brilliant white light flashed behind his eyes, then winked out into total darkness, and he felt himself fall into a black, bottomless pit.

Chapter 5

Gray. Cool gray. Ki could feel the airy coolness first as consciousness returned. Then, as he cracked open his eyes, he could see the opaque grayness of false dawn overhead. Next came sensations of movement and sound...the rumbling of wheels, the creaking shift of wood, the bumping roll of someone pressing alongside him.

Finally, Ki grew fully aware of his surroundings. He was stretched flat in the splintery bed of an old farm wagon, his arms bound behind him, wrists and ankles tied by what seemed like rawhide thongs. He felt dizzy and disoriented, and was stabbed by pain each time the wagon bounced and smacked its bed-boards against the base of his skull.

Whatever had struck him unconscious, had struck him there; it was a tender, raw spot, and Ki turned his head, preferring to have an ear hammered instead. He found himself staring directly at Jessie, who was lying close beside him, similarly tied and on her back.

"Good morning," she whispered. "Sleep well?"

"What a dumb—"

"Shh, keep it low. No need for them to hear us."

Twisting, using the wagon's sway to help, Ki maneuvered so he could peer forward. To the left, a faint, luminous wash was seeping along the eastern horizon, but dimness still clung to the land, obscuring the two small, slim figures hunched on the spring seat. Their backs were to him, and the driver was further shadowed by a wide-brimmed anthill sombrero. The other was veiled by a less impressive hat and a bulky wool jacket, but posture and graceful motion alone were enough for Ki to identify Evita. Evita of the winsome guile and the knockout punch.

Ki slumped, disgusted. "So they suckered you too, Jessie."

"Not the same way they did you, I gather. Two men leveled guns at me, after a commotion in the hall woke me and I went to investigate. There they were, and the pair in front, who were arguing by your door."

"Neat ruse, making you think I needed help in a squabble."

"Oh, it was genuine. They were arguing about having to dress you. The man—the third man, the one driving now—kept calling the girl a *puta*. She kept insisting she'd done only what was absolutely necessary to catch you off guard, until he slapped her and she started crying."

"I'd have liked to hear that. Shame I wasn't there."

"You were, drenching wet and trussed like a Christmas goose."

"Ah, she must've hit me with the water pitcher."

"Then they sneaked us out a rear door, and here we are."

"Dressed, at least, though it's a wonder."

"I'm more curious to know why we're alive," Jessie said.

The wagon crunched into a pothole, sending both of them lurching. Ki, banging his rib cage, suddenly noticed that his daggers and *shuriken* were still in his vest. "One good thing about their argument—it distracted them from searching my clothes. What about you? Any weapons?"

"Not my pistol, of course, but I was able to slip along the derringer. Just the girl guarded me and, ah, honored my modesty while I dressed. But y'know," Jessie mused, "I believe she would've shot."

"Did she threaten you?"

"More the look in her eyes. She apologized, actually, for her actions with *'mi compadre, el matón,'* but she said it was better to soil the hands so that one may have the chance to wash the whole body later."

"Called it her hands, did she? Called me a tough, eh?" Ki grinned a tight, feral, humorless grin. "Where are the other two men?"

"Riding behind."

"Can they see us?"

"I doubt it, not while we're lying down. Why?"

"El matón is going to work loose and then free you."

Ki sounded convinced that he could, and Jessie felt confident of it. She'd watched him practicing, purposely disjointing his bones until he'd wriggle eellike out of ropes, chains, all sorts of bonds. She also had a good idea what Ki planned to do afterward: silently dispose of the riders, then tackle the driver and the girl.

She shook her head. "They took us alive and they're taking us somewhere, for some reason. Wait a while, and let's try to find out more."

"All right," Ki acceded, and lapsed quiet, resting. . . .

The wagon trundled on at a snail's pace. Soon the

sky glowed brassily, the sun rising crimson and swollen. Ki remained silently relaxing while the increasingly warm rays soothed his aching head. Jessie was the first to stir, struggling to sit upright and restore what circulation she could, and to try to figure where they were.

The landscape was a rugged vista of arroyos, mesas, boulders, and sand, a sprawling desert waste sparsely grown with prickly pear, barrel cactus, and scarlet-streaming ocotillo. Ahead and a bit to her left, she could glimpse a forbidding series of steppelike plateaus escalating to a not-so-distant phalanx of lofty pinnacles and craggy gorges—the crests and canyons, she sensed, of the Portrillo Mountains.

The girl, glancing back, said, *"Bueno,"* and reached under the seat for a battered canteen. She clambered into the bed. "Please, nothing foolish. My father promises to shoot."

The driver turned, a venerable Enfield rifle across his lap, and straddled the seat so he could keep an eye on the prisoners. He mainly kept his eye, a glowering eye, on Ki.

Ki rose, caustic. "Pleased to meet you, Señor De Baca."

Evita glanced at her father, then at Ki, then hastily held the canteen to Jessie's lips. "I'm Evita, *sí,"* she said, and she sounded embarrassed. "But this is my true father, Cardenas Torres."

Jessie drank slowly, thoroughly wetting her mouth before swallowing. Cardenas Torres sat mutely, but his expression was sufficient to reveal an abiding, paternal desire to blow a .577-caliber hole through Ki. And Ki, in a mocking echo of last night, said,

70

"Evita, surely he's as you swore, the heroic and pro-lific Don Felipe, he of seven and a half *niños.*"

"Don't scorn me," Evita snapped, thrusting the canteen from Jessie to Ki. "You're not so smart or holy. If you'd had religion instead of passion, you'd have known I couldn't attend school in Santa Fe. The only college there is St. Michael's, for boys."

Jessie almost burst out laughing. But Ki's cha-grined expression made her hurriedly switch subjects. "Tell me, where are we going?"

Torres answered for his daughter. "There," he said, pointing to the mountain range ahead. "One camp of *Los Renegados,* our people."

"Is that where De Baca and Harrigan were taken?"

Both shrugged; if they knew, they weren't telling.

Undaunted, Jessica demanded, "But why have your people, as you call them, been raiding and killing, and now kidnapping across the border?"

Torres spat over the edge of the wagon, an expan-sive gesture of contempt in a country lacking water. "Listen to her! She's like all *gringos,* soft and forgetful of what it takes to win a *revolution.*"

"I remember that our revolt was in America, and yours is supposed to be in Mexico. What we may be doesn't excuse your attacking us up here."

"Excuse? Pah!" Evita exclaimed sharply. "We don't need to make excuses, only sacrifices, when strug-gling for our freedom."

"Sacrifices like the one you made last night?" Ki asked.

Evita stiffened, her black eyes stormy. *"Federales,* Señor Ki, much like the *soldados* who died in Mos-quero, murdered my mother after . . . using her." She

71

averted her face. "I pity but don't regret their deaths, just as I am sorry but not ashamed of having tricked you."

"Enough, Evita," her father growled. "We were warned not to speak to these gringos. It's wrong to have even offered them water."

"Why us? Why have we been taken?" Jessie asked.

Evita, her head bowed, moved toward the seat. "I follow orders."

"*Sí, silencio!*" Torres slapped his Enfield for emphasis.

Ki opened his mouth to bait Evita again—to provoke her into blurting out more than she should—but then decided to give it a rest. Grudgingly, he had to admire the little vixen. He'd been around enough to have been plied by other women for various reasons. Yet Evita had played it pretty slick; he'd thought for a while that she really was De Baca's daughter. Her seeming sincerity was apparently due to a deep belief that her cause justified her means.

Before settling down again, Ki took a moment to gaze about, squinting in the harsh glare of angling sunlight. Midmorning, he judged. The two horsemen tagging a short distance behind the wagon were a coarse and swarthy pair, straw-hatted, bristling with weapons and sporting "prairie" cartridge belts. Ki felt more antagonism toward them than he did toward Evita. They were typical of a breed he'd met before on both sides of the border: Clean-shaven or whiskered, fancy-clad or in rags, they were common thugs motivated by greed, not oppressed peons driven to extremes. Cardenas Torres and Evita—for all her enticing and calf-eyed deception—were obviously idealists. Too bad their vision was so blinding. . . .

The wagon continued its lumbering creep. The rumpled, tawny gray flatlands became rugged, wind-swept foothills, and those in time became a ravaged panorama of buttes and gorges. Breathing deeply, the wagon's horse slowed to a plodding walk as the trail wound higher, through a labyrinth of wooded slopes, jagged hogbacks, and stony ridges.

Suddenly, as they angled around a doglegged shoulder, a voice rang out from a dark ledge above: *"Quién vive?"*

Torres cupped his mouth. *"El Grito*—the Insurrection!"

"Pasa."

Torres flipped the reins and the wagon jounced forward. A hundred yards farther on, all trace of the sentry was gone. The sun was a now a white, searing ingot directly overhead. It was noon, nine or nine and a half hours since they'd left Mosquero. They must be twenty to twenty-five miles southeast of the town, Jessie estimated, which would definitely place them somewhere up in the Portrillos.

There was one bend after another, one sharp dip or rise followed by still more curves, as the wagon twisted upward through a rocky canyon. Eventually they came to a narrow cleft between towering cliffs, and after passing through the gap, Jessie saw that they were on the wall of a vast depression shaped like a huge bowl. Water could be heard trickling in the near distance, and a small creek snaked through the middle of the bowl. Around the water grew sparse grass, and where it collected into a pool, there rose a few scraggly cottonwoods and cedars.

The wagon descended into the bowl, heading toward a clearing close by the trees. Grouped about the clearing were bedrolls and crude tents, smoldering cookfires, stacks of rifles and scattered equipment, and a loose cavvy of horses and mules. There were no pickets, no emplacements, not even a crude perimeter of stakes, only the ring of hills to serve as a defense. Whatever else the camp was, it was not military-minded.

Upwards of fifty men and a handful of women could be seen lazing or working. A few appeared to be Mexican peasants, like Cardenas and Evita Torres, responding to a call for liberty. Most looked akin to the two riders who'd accompanied them, using the crusade as a license to plunder and kill—which, Jessica realized, didn't necessarily mean Renegado's revolt was unjust or false. Perhaps this camp was such a remote extension of his main force that Renegado was unaware of who was in it. Or perhaps he knew, and they were the sort he wanted...

The wagon drew to a halt in front of a large canvas wall tent. Obviously this would be the headquarters of the camp leader, the *caudillo* behind the traps, abductions, and slaughters on American soil. Jessie and Ki tensed expectantly as Torres jumped down from the wagon and walked toward the tent. The two riders dismounted and hurried to stop him before he could enter, one pushing him away while the other ducked under the tent flap. He reappeared with the leader.

Ignoring Torres, the camp leader strode to the wagon bed and gazed in at Jessie and Ki. He was dressed in clothing similar to that of his men, but he was loaded down with two separate shell belts and holstered revolvers. *"Buenas tardes,"* he greeted them affably. "Nice to see you again."

The man was Don Felipe De Baca.

Jessie and Ki stared incredulously.

"Come, you can't be shocked speechless," De Baca chided them.

Tight-lipped, Jessie replied, "Almost. I'm stunned to think you sat dining and joking with your own loyal honor guard, knowing the whole time that you'd sentenced them to be slaughtered."

He shrugged. "A soldier's duty is to die."

"And us; and Harrigan too, if he'd been along."

"Regrettable, but unavoidable."

"You're a cold-blooded bastard," Ki said thinly. "People must be very stupid or naïve to believe you— to make sacrifices for you."

De Baca shrugged nonchalantly. Evita, at whom Ki's barb had also been aimed, seemed to flinch slightly, though her expression remained grim with determination. It was her father who reacted most wrathfully, leaping to a rear wheel hub, leaning in, and savagely backhanding Ki.

"Depravado!" Torres snarled. "How dare you hurl insults!"

De Baca laughed, then brusquely cuffed Torres off the wagon. *"Lárgarte!"* he snapped, and turned to Evita. "Quick, *amor mio,* a meal for our guests." Finally he ordered the two riders, "Bring our guests to the fire."

The wagon's tailgate was lowered, and Jessie and Ki were harshly hauled out. They dropped to their knees, their legs cramped from lack of circulation, and were dragged across to the nearest campfire.

Then one of the men, anticipating De Baca, has-

75

tened into the tent and returned with a folding stool. "I'm to tell you that he'll be out momentarily," the man reported. *"De acuerdo?"*

De Baca nodded, sitting down on the stool, and waved both men away. Evita and her father lingered somewhat closer; they huddled twenty yards away at a smaller but more active cookfire, Torres stoking the blaze while Evita began preparing food.

De Baca took a thin cheroot from his shirt pocket, and in a soft, amused voice said to Ki, "So. You must've romped with Evita. Her father's very excitable when he learns of it, but ah! she's a passionate *chingada, verdad?"* His question was rhetorical; without waiting for an answer, he fired his cheroot with a piece of kindling and sat back, chuckling.

Jessie asked sharply, "Why've you had us brought here? You tried killing us two or three times, so why've you abducted us now?"

"For good reason, Señorita Starbuck. I didn't think of this when I'd ordered you and Ki disposed of, but I'm glad now that the attempts failed. You are, it turns out, much more valuable alive."

"For a while."

"Sí, for a while."

"That still doesn't answer my question."

"You'll learn soon enough. Be patient."

"What about Renegado? Does he know what you're doing?"

"Renegado is a *baboso*—a fool."

"In other words, he doesn't know. Yet he must be aware of your hideout here, of your raiding on our side of the border."

"Of course, and he approves. Such raids help to weaken Diaz."

76

"But why go to the trouble of kidnapping yourself?"

"To stir up official anger, Jessie," Ki suggested. "Mexico gets angry because our government couldn't protect its envoy, and Washington gets angry because Mexicans invaded us so blatantly. It spoils any hope of the governments calming their people and working together. What I don't understand, De Baca, is how you're figuring to explain riding into Mexico, alive and free, leading your captors."

"I'll simply pretend to have escaped from here," De Baca explained smoothly. "I'll join Renegado's main force in Chihuahua, and if and when I'm asked, I'll explain that these men here were bandits—"

"Which they are."

"Whether they are or not, I'll denounce them as bandits, not true followers of Renegado. But that'll be a minor point, readily overlooked in the war which by then will have broken out."

"You want retaliation? You want hatred and conflict?"

"It will be a war Mexico cannot possibly win, *verdad?* So it'll be an unpopular war, and seem to stem from Diaz's stupid, ineffective policies. The masses will flock to Renegado, who is one of their own."

"And after Diaz's overthrow, you overthrow Renegado."

"Astute, Señorita, more astute than Renegado has been. He doesn't foresee the war, nor the need for a man skilled in diplomacy to end it. Taking over in a coup in order to sue for peace will establish me as a wise and benevolent *presidente* in the eyes of both our peoples."

"And the entire time you're being hailed as the

Savior of Mexico, you and your gang will be robbing it blind. How loathsome."

De Baca laughed smugly. "Even if you're right, no one will know or be able to do anything about it. I'll be too firmly in power. The name of Don Felipe De Baca will be on the lips of every citizen, will be praised in the streets, will be blessed in every prayer."

"And somehow we figure in your evil scheme. How?"

Another voice answered Jessie; a voice with a thick, guttural purr, like the throaty growl of a feline predator. "Allow me to respond, Señor De Baca. It's time my friends learned of their fate."

"The Iceman!" Jessie gasped.

"Von Eismann, *bitte*," he corrected, approaching from the tent. "I do not call you names, much as I may wish to."

The German was six-foot-plus, more than two hundred pounds of solid muscle, and wore an expensive fawn-brown shirt, butternut twill pants, and "mule-ear" boots with long-roweled spurs. Against the sun-tanned flesh of his Prussian features, his short-cropped, pale blond hair appeared hoarfrost-white, the same color as his eyebrows, which angled up from the bridge of his broken nose, then slanted down sharply over frigid blue eyes.

Ki strained in his bonds. "But I saw you—"

"Die? *Nein*, you saw me ride over a cliff. At dusk, a time of shadows and contrasts. Me, I saw a small ledge, a tree..." He made a grabbing motion with his left hand. "I leaped and caught hold..."

The Iceman's left hand was gloved in black pigskin, with razorlike talons protruding from its fingertips. The hand was more than merely artificial; it was mechanical, capable of opening and closing—and, as Jessie and Ki knew all too well, of bludgeoning and strangling.

Ki eyed the hand and its owner with open hatred. He'd always felt suspicious of Von Eismann's plunge into that abyss, but his own injuries then had prevented him from checking thoroughly. Now, here was confirmation that Von Eismann was the calculating schemer he'd believed him to be, rather than a quitter who'd commit suicide to avoid capture. Worse, both Ki and Jessie knew Von Eismann to be a callous assassin for the cartel, the ruthless European crime ring they'd dedicated their lives to destroy. The Iceman's presence could only mean that the syndicate was involved with De Baca's treachery—and by extension, with Renegado's war-threatening revolution.

"Normally I wouldn't have interfered with Señor De Baca's plans," Von Eismann continued. "Then I learned it was you whose deaths he wanted, and suggested a more appropriate ending for you, one suitable to your prominence. Consider yourselves honored; you're to be the key figures in one of the two final incidents which will ignite the war."

"Never!"

"Willing or unwilling, Fräulein Starbuck, it doesn't matter. The fact remains that in a couple of days, an important official in Diaz's government will be shot—a man who distrusts Señor De Baca, and opposed his appointment as envoy. You'll be there too, to take the blame."

"Nobody'd believe I'd murder a Mexican official!"

"But they will." The rider who'd fetched the stool for De Baca now brought one for Von Eismann, but the German waved the man aside, preferring to stand

79

over the prisoners. "It'll appear as if you left Mosquero on your own, for Mexico City. And it'll be
rumored that you became crazed, killing mad, vowing
to avenge the deaths of your congressmen and Secretary of War, and everyone else aboard the train."

"What?"

"*Sí*, the train will not be arriving in Mosquero,"
De Baca added with blatant relish. "It will be blown
up as it crosses the trestle at Purgatory Gorge, and
my men will be there to handle any survivors."

Jessie was shocked speechless, appalled by the
wholesale butchery that Von Eismann and De Baca
were plotting. Purgatory Gorge was deep in the Florida Mountains, and was so named because the original
builders had perished when the trestle, half completed,
had unexpectedly collapsed. Their bones were still to
be found scattered among the rocks at the bottom of
the treacherous chasm. If De Baca and his gang dy-
namited the spindly trestle just as the congressional
party was crossing over it, and then picked off any
who might live through the fall, not a passenger on
board could possibly escape death.

She happened to glance past De Baca, and saw that
Cardenas Torres had left the other fire, where Evita
was squatting, frying some scraps of meat. The older
man was edging closer to De Baca and Von Eismann,
apparently searching for more firewood; but the immediate area had long since been scoured of tree
branches and limbs, and Cardenas seemed more intent
on overhearing conversation than on finding scarce
kindling.

A glimmer of an idea occurred to Jessie then. If
she could get De Baca or Von Eismann to say something incriminating while Torres was within earshot,

it might be enough to jar the man into responding. As loyal to Mexico as Torres seemed to be, he might rashly break in, angrily berating De Baca, possibly even struggling with him. If he did, if he caused enough of an uproar, the diversion might allow Ki a chance to escape. Assuming that Ki could manage to free himself.

Nudging Ki, she whispered, "You've waited long enough."

Ki gave a nod. He too had noticed Torres sidling nearer, as though drawn by curiosity; Von Eismann, apparently unaware that many Mexicans knew at least a smattering of English, had been bragging loudly of plans best kept secret from honest, if misguided, patriots. And, like Jessie, Ki wanted to take advantage of the Iceman's mistaken boasting. So even before Jessie's whispered retraction of her previous order not to act, Ki had been starting to slip out of the rawhide thongs.

Slowly he dislocated the bones of his wrists and hands. He realized bleakly that with each pop of a joint, each stretch of a tendon, he might be helping to kill Jessie—but it was an execution to which she had knowingly sentenced herself by her whisper. They both knew how slim his chances were of escaping alone, and how impossible it might be to release her as well during any momentary confusion. He might have to leave Jessica behind, to face certain retribution. The odds, even then, were greatly against Ki, for he'd be pursued by skilled hunters familiar with these mountains, and should he elude them, he'd still have a rocky, arid wasteland to cross before he'd reach help.

Yet both were determined to try, however they had

81

to. And if they failed, as most likely they would, then they must try again, and again. Every minute that passed made it that much harder, and once they broke camp, every minute would send them that much farther away, as De Baca took them south to Mexico City—to a rendezvous with death, and a resultant conflict that would kill thousands.

Jessie waited until Torres had edged to within a few feet of them, and then asked, "How are you planning to dispose of Renegado?"

Von Eismann laughed. "Why worry?"

"Oh, I'm not worrying. It's just that I'm like you, Von Eismann; I like all the details to be nailed down ahead of time."

"An admirable trait, Fräulein! *Sehr gut!* If it'll satisfy you, we have uses for Renegado not dissimilar to the ones we have for you."

"I see. So you're going to kill him. Well, you can't afford to have him around after you overthrow him, I imagine, in case the people wish him back. What's it to be? Put him up against a wall?"

Not wishing to stare obviously, lest Von Eismann and De Baca grow suspicious, Jessica glanced peripherally at Torres, seeing him stop as if frozen. Clearly, Torres had heard the exchange, and his face was etched with shock as he stared at De Baca's broad back.

De Baca now laughed, his own voice rising dramatically. "A firing squad for a national hero? You joke!"

"Yes, how silly of me. Perhaps a setup like you're planning for us? Another assassination by a crazy gringo?"

"Bah! To do such would only increase the war

fervor between our countries, and make it harder for me to step in and negotiate peace."

"No sabotage, then; that'd cause internal dissension." Jessie appeared to be thinking hard. "A convenient accident, it has to be."

"*Sí*, a most tragic one. Renegado will die a martyr," De Baca declared, "thus cementing my position and my politics with the people. There's nothing better for strengthening a cause, *no es verdad?*"

"Gold and power, those are your only causes," Jessie retorted, abruptly turning furious. "You don't care about your people at all!"

"I care about myself! Do you not have a saying in this country, Señorita, about the people getting the government they deserve?"

"We vote ours in, and we can vote it out. Your people are fighting to get Renegado, and are unaware they'll be getting you—a puppet of a foreign criminal power more vicious than any Mexican *bandido* gang."

"What of it? I'll be getting the *vivas,* the bowing and scraping of brainless ones who'll grovel to do my every bidding!"

"Like the Torreses?"

"Like them, *sí, muy estúpido*—"

Suddenly a bellow of rage erupted behind De Baca, and Cardenas Torres hurtled forward, his features contorted, his gnarled peasant's hands bunched into fists. De Baca and Von Eismann swung around, De Baca upsetting his stool as he staggered upright to fend off Torres. Ki tried frantically to pull his hands loose, needing just another minute, a half a minute, more to wriggle free.

"Traitor!" Torres shouted, punching and clawing De Baca. "Filthy *guarro!* The Anglos were right! I'll kill you with my bare hands!"

De Baca swung an elbow brutally into the man's ribs, sending him stumbling backward into Von Eismann. Ki wormed one limp, seemingly boneless hand through, the rawhide loops drooping...but he was too late.

With the speed of a cobra, Von Eismann slid his right hand up under Torres's sombrero and over his hand, sinking his fingers into the man's eye sockets for a firm grip. He wrenched back while, simultaneously, his metal left hand grabbed Torres by the scruff of the neck and shoved forward. The snap of Torres's cracking spine was like that of a hatchet splitting green wood.

Released, Torres collapsed, instantaneously dead. Evita screamed, horrified, from the other campfire, *"Papá! Madre de Dios, Papá!"* She dropped her skillet and ran to her father and flung herself down beside him and cradled his flopping head to her bosom, her soft hair covering both of them like a shroud as she sobbed abjectly.

Jessie felt sickened. When she'd conceived of the idea to pit Torres against De Baca, it had never occurred to her that the unarmed old patriot might be slain. She glanced at Ki, tears involuntarily welling in her eyes. He shook his head, his face grim and hostile; his hands were both free now, but he wisely kept them hidden while he clicked the bones back into joint. The time, this time, was past.

"It was inevitable, Jessie," he told her in a low, comforting voice. "Sooner or later Torres would've caught on to the truth, and would've reacted the same way, with undoubtedly the same outcome."

De Baca went to Evita. "I'm sorry, *querida.*"

"*Ja,* your father attacked us," Von Eismann said, arrogantly indignant. "We were forced to defend ourselves, you could see that."

Evita didn't answer him. She kept moaning softly, embracing her dead father. Jessie and Ki held their tongues, sensing the futility of further words, and fearing to endanger the girl now. A long silence ensued. At last Evita lowered the body to the ground, and stood staring dry-eyed at De Baca and Von Eismann.

"Yes, you're right. I cannot blame you," she said humbly. "Perhaps my father lost his head from strain. But he has not died in vain. *El Grito* will triumph!" She glanced from De Baca down to her father. "The salvation of our people is worth any price."

Jessie felt a sinking sensation in the pit of her stomach. She slumped wearily, feeling hopeless of ever escaping, of saving the congressional party, of stopping two nations from declaring war.

Chapter 6

Von Eismann and De Baca smiled with self-assurance that bordered on contempt. Then Von Eismann turned to De Baca, saying, "Shouldn't we be going? You told me by noon at latest, and here it is..."

His ominous tone was sufficient to whip De Baca into action. "*Sí*, at once. It was merely because of all that's been happening—" De Baca pivoted to address his men, who'd been gathering like vultures around Torres's corpse. "*Ándale, piojos*, load the wagons! We must leave now, to reach the gorge by daybreak!"

There was a flurry of activity. Two rickety wagons were rolled over to where a canvas tarpaulin covered several wooden crates. These were lifted into the wagon beds and tied down firmly, while teams were hitched and saddlehorses split from the cavvy. Apparently most of the men were to ride with De Baca, Jessie saw; the few left behind were of peasant stock like Torres, zealous but basically decent, who mightn't be trusted to massacre wantonly. De Baca was taking no chances. And backed by forty-odd unscrupulous killers and two wagonloads of explosives, De Baca was also taking no chances that anyone aboard the congressional train would survive his ambush at Purgatory Gorge.

Nor, for that matter, was he taking chances with Jessie and Ki. He detailed the rider who'd fetched the stools to remain in camp and guard them—and prob-

86

ably to keep an eye as well on Torres's peasant compatriots. Evita persuaded two of the peons to carry her father to the bank of the pool, where they laid him, wrapped in a tattered blanket, for burial. Jessie overheard them telling Evita that they'd dig a grave later, after De Baca and his crew had left; she couldn't help wondering how any woman could be so devoted in her beliefs as to excuse, even venerate, her father's murderers. Perhaps Evita would break down later . . . but later would be too late.

Evita returned alone to the little cookfire and retrieved her skillet. She hunkered down, lips taut, her face an expressionless mask, eyes averted as De Baca ordered his men and wagons to proceed.

Von Eismann and De Baca rode out, leading their party, and the Iceman inclined his head toward Jessie in a sardonic Prussian bow as he trotted past. Angry and frustrated, she gazed at them winding out of the camp, up the trail to the narrow cleft, and out of view.

A lethargic hush fell over the camp. Torres was buried, a few kind words were murmured, then his mourners and gravediggers resumed their lazy puttering or dozing in the shade. The remaining animals tethered in the cavvy stood with heads lowered, as though dozing afoot. Only the guard appeared unable to relax, and was walking restlessly about, his left hand clutching a .50-70 Springfield repeater, his right hand either resting on the butt of his holstered Starr .44, or holding a dirty cup of stale coffee.

The blazing white sun descended toward midafternoon. Evita, who was seemingly immersed in her cooking as some form of therapy, stirred from the fire only long enough to fetch more meat; then she squatted on her heels again, frying the fresh chunks, the animal fat sizzling and smoking fragrantly. The guard—a swarthy *mestizo* with a pockmarked face and a barrel chest—was evidently pissed off at having to stay behind, and kept on pacing, scowling and cursing at everyone around.

Ki said to Jessie, "Tonight, after dark."

"I suppose," Jessica sighed. "Are you loose?"

"My hands are. I can't free my feet without being seen."

"No talking!" the guard demanded, menacing them with his rifle.

They fell silent, not wanting to attract the guard's attention—attention that could lead to his discovery of Ki's freed hands. They sat quietly watching, edginess growing within them, perversely urging them to act now, before night came to conceal their moves.

Evita continued cooking. The sunlight made a pale wash of her face, subduing its grief-stricken expression; she looked very young and very proud, and very much hewn out of stone. The guard continued his prowling, alert to the slightest motion or sound. Then, during one of his restive circuits over to check the cavvy, Evita rose, took a wooden spoon, and casually walked with the sizzling pan toward Jessie.

The guard hastened back. "Hey! What're you doing?"

"Feeding them."

"Don't! Take it back, *niña.*"

"Don Felipe himself ordered this food for them."

The two faced each other adamantly.

"Do you wish to follow my father, Miguel?" Evita snapped defiantly. "And look, these *tontos* are tied up, harmless. You risk more by making me disobey Don Felipe than by letting me feed them."

The guard muttered, indecisive. Finally, frowning, he growled, *"Bueno,* but be quick about it."

Turning, Evita strolled the rest of the way to Jessie. "It's badger meat," she said as she knelt. "I'm sorry there's not more."

Jessie shook her head. "I'm not hungry."

"Eat anyway." Evita prompted her with the spoon, shifting closer beside Jessie. "And chew slowly."

Jessie ate, finding it necessary to chew slowly; the meat was leather-tough and so hot that it burnt her mouth. The guard stood back, and Jessie could tell by their positions that he couldn't quite see the skillet in Evita's lap, or her other hand nearly touching Jessie's thigh. The guard watched them nonetheless, suspiciously at first, then with increasing nervousness as the spooning and chewing went on interminably. At last, bored and aggravated, the guard sauntered off.

Almost immediately, Jessie felt the cold, thin blade of a knife easing around behind her, and down her arm. "Evita . . ."

"Not a word, not one word. Just eat."

While Evita kept on feeding her with one hand, she blindly maneuvered the knife with the other. When the blade finally slid between her bound wrists, Jessie began moving her hands in rhythm to Evita's sawing. The rawhide started parting.

Evita grimaced. "I never thought it'd come to this."

"To you helping us, or to your father being murdered?"

"Murder, *asesinato,* a terrible word in any language."

"Well, do you know any word that fits better?"

Evita didn't respond, didn't meet her eyes. She changed positions, letting her *camisa* drape over Jes-

89

sie's legs so that she could work on the thongs around her ankles. Again, the actions of feeding and eating masked the surreptitious cutting, though her new position made Evita more vulnerable to the scrutiny of the guard.

The guard was returning. Suddenly, Evita stood up and spat at Jessie. "Pig! You slobbered on me, made me spill!" She turned angrily to Ki, squatting alongside him as she had Jessica. "Don't you be drooling on me, or you'll get nothing!" she warned loudly.

The guard laughed and, distracted by Evita's outburst, failed to see how the rawhide on Jessie's ankles was merely draped in place. He watched awhile, then grunted and moved on. Once more Evita slipped her knife out from beneath the skillet, preparing to release Ki's wrists.

"Just my feet," Ki murmured. "My hands are already free."

"I should've guessed," Evita grumbled softly, thrusting the spoon into Ki's mouth as she shifted to get at the thongs around his ankles. "If there's a way to get out of something, you'd find it."

Ki smiled thinly, and when Evita took her spoon back, he said, "Maybe, but so far you're the only one doing anything to get out."

"Am I?" Evita looked up at Ki with blank eyes, which made her response all the more puzzling to him. But before Ki could ask her what she meant, before she'd even managed to slice all the way through the rawhide, the guard realized they were up to no good.

He ran forward, swinging his rifle to bear. "That'll do, *niña!* Get away, before I shoot—"

Evita whirled and slung the skillet at him. It struck

his shoulder, and the burning grease and hot bits of meat splashed and scalded his face; he threw up his hands, dropping the rifle as he clawed his eyes, screaming.

Jessie straightened, kicking off the cut rawhide thongs. Ki rolled, trying to stand but still hobbled by the thongs; he wrenched at them with his hands, and they parted. Both he and Jessie stumbled, lack of circulation making their legs feel prickly and cumbersome.

"Hurry!" Evita cried. "To the horses, before—"

But the screaming of the guard had already roused the camp. Evita snatched up the guard's rifle, then scrambled toward the horses. Jessie and Ki followed in awkward, lunging runs. The yells of the men rushing to intercept them, the howls of the guard, and the nervous whinnying of the horses created a confused din. Shots were fired.

There was no time for stealth. Bullets snarled around the three as they dashed across the open clearing, only Evita's erratic rifle fire keeping the pursuers at bay, off stride and off target. Then Ki swiveled, crouching, flinging *shuriken* at the oncoming men, his whirling disks stabbing one in the chest and ripping through the throat of another. Joining in, Jessie fired one barrel of her two-shot derringer, dropping a third man with a slug in his belly.

The initial charge scattered, and in the bloody tumult, the trio reached the remuda. Evita cut the main picket rope as Jessie threw herself on a claybank mare. Guns blazed to bring her down, but Evita fired her rifle twice more, sending the men diving for cover, while allowing Jessie time to heel the mare into a hard gallop back through the clearing.

Ki was a split second behind, swinging onto a deep-brisketed bay gelding. A handful of the camp's men rallied and attacked with a broadside of bullets. Ki paused for an instant, waiting for Evita to mount. Instead, slapping and shouting, she deliberately stampeded all the rest of the horses and mules. Spooked, eyes rolling, they bolted toward the advancing men, who scurried abruptly aside.

And Ki, in that sudden moment, realized what Evita had meant by her enigmatic comment just before. "I won't let you," he muttered, and leaning over, one hand entwined in his horse's mane, he scooped Evita up while he kicked the gelding harshly in the ribs.

Evita struggled, only to lose her rifle and be swept off her feet as Ki's horse surged forward, while around and behind them roared a barrage of gunfire. Clinging precariously and clutching Evita about her slim waist, Ki bent low against the bay's neck and urged it on faster, as they crossed the deadly gantlet of the exposed clearing.

"Let go!" Evita kept squealing. "Let me go!"

"You'll go—with us!" Ki retorted. "You're not going to get us out by purposely getting yourself killed!"

Evita gave a throaty sob and sagged in Ki's embracing arm. Riding furiously, they followed Jessie as bullets cracked from the regrouping camp. The trail grew steeper. Ahead loomed the gap in the cliff. A shot plucked at Ki's vest; another seared a welt across the bay's rump, making it rear, almost unseating Ki and Evita.

Then they were into the cleft, and the guns could no longer seek them out. Ki figured they had a short breathing space, perhaps as much as half an hour's head start, depending on how quickly the camp personnel could round up the horses and mount a chase. But ahead of them was the sentry, certain to be forewarned and alarmed by the commotion.

"Jessie!" Ki yelled. "Jessie, slow down!"

She reined in, allowing Ki and Evita to close the few yards separating them, the bay gelding lathered and panting from its double load. "Thank heavens," she said breathlessly. "You made it."

"Nearly didn't," Ki replied, eyeing Evita darkly. "Señorita Sacrifice here was bent on helping us, but not herself."

"It was *my* only way out," Evita said miserably, as Ki boosted her up behind him. "I was—I am—in too deep."

"No deeper right now than we are," Jessie responded, refusing to cater to the girl's melancholy. "Can you guide us out of these mountains, Evita, and back to Mosquero?"

Evita nodded, and they set off at a rapid trot.

Without her, retracing their path would have been dangerously time-consuming and difficult. They would emerge from one spur, only to cross a rock-strewn shelf that would lead to yet another scrub-clogged hollow, their route a deceptive linkage of many trails, some intersecting and others separated by trackless stone benches. The farther they rode, the more like a maze it became, while the sun continued its slow decline, gilding the far peaks to their right.

Gradually the broad canyon drew in, its slopes rising higher and nearer, becoming sheer cliffs funneling toward a narrow defile—the entry to a section of shoulder that Ki recalled vividly from that morning.

He called a halt. "The sentry's just ahead."

"Shall we make a run for it?"

"I'd hate to try, Jessie. If you remember, it's a bottleneck there, with a long bare patch beyond, and the sentry's liable to be roosting with a scoped rifle. We'd be prime targets."

"Then I guess we'll have to go around."

"Imposible," Evita answered Jessica. "Short of climbing and hiking overland, this is the only passage to or from the camp."

Ki asked, "How does the sentry get up to his perch?"

Evita thought for a moment, then replied, "There's a small path in the hill, like steps mounting up to the ledge where he stays."

"Show me."

Two minutes later, Evita indicated where a slender thread of a path led around a massive granite boulder and up the rock face. Nearby, a saddled pinto—evidently the sentry's horse—looked up disinterestedly, then resumed nuzzling a crop of dried yellow grass.

Ki dismounted, gesturing for the two women to remain on horseback while he surveyed the path. It was, as Evita had said, hardly more than a set of stairs and winding ridges hacked in along the wall, rising steeply to disappear over the crest high above. It was strictly a single-file ascent, with one misstep enough to send a person hurtling to his death; and worse, the sentry would certainly hear and probably see any approach long before he could be gotten to.

"Stay put," he told them. "I'll go on alone."

"But—"

"The path's a deathtrap, Jessie. I'm going to have to sneak up some other place." Then Ki grinned reassuringly at Evita. "Don't look so glum. We just found you a horse and gear, didn't we? Why don't you shorten the pinto's stirrup leathers while I'm gone, so they'll fit those legs of yours. We'll be riding as soon as I'm back."

"If you get back, you . . . you *feto!"*

Ki's grin widened as he turned away. "I'm not a twit, Evita, I'm a *matón,* a tough. Or have you forgotten already?"

He walked along the rock-littered base of the slope, studying it with thoughtful care. For a good hundred yards he couldn't find a spot that didn't require a rope to scale. He kept on searching, moving into the defile, seeing that in the first bend of the dogleg shoulder, the possibilities for ascent were slightly better. As he drew closer, he scrutinized the apex of the wall that thrust out into the bend, figuring the trail he'd have to climb, mapping each jutting ledge and handhold in his memory. He must make no mistake, no false start.

Gripping his first handhold with steady fingers, Ki began his climb. Forty feet from the trail, he gained a thrusting projection no wider than his hand, but it served as a foothold, and he paused to rest a moment and flex his fingers. A horizontal niche ran almost alongside him for twenty feet or more, toward his left.

Like a persistent, slow-creeping beetle, Ki worked along this crevice, clinging by his hands. He reached the broken apex of the shoulder and climbed another forty feet, using his fingers and toes. Straddling a sliver of rock that stuck outward like a stubby horn, he rested, viewing both angles of the defile below. Even here, his range of vision along the serpentine trail was limited.

Gazing upward, he saw that he must trust to luck,

or else spend time hunting out a possible detour. But time, right now, was scarcer than luck. Ki continued straight upward, hand over hand, slowly, smoothly, so that no jerk or unbalanced shift would cause him to slip. Strangely, he sensed the tug of unseen eyes upon him. Yet he saw nothing on or near the frowning rim above, as, with sweat trickling into his eyes, he continued to gradually raise himself, clinging with the strength of one hand while exploring with the other.

With a weary sigh, he reached a point where the shoulder slanted inward. He rested, then climbed onward, faster, but after a few moments the cliff face straightened again to form another wall. This one last high step, he judged, would bring him to the top. He searched the ragged lip of the rim, still feeling vaguely that he was being watched, and still unable to find any reason for it. He shrugged it off, concentrating on the short section remaining. He estimated that his best hold on the rim would be a plate of stone, cut away on either side and sticking out like a balcony, above him and a little to the right.

"So far, so good," he murmured, hoisting himself upward.

A toe of a boot appeared at the edge of the stone slab.

Ki stopped.

There was a scraping of boot leather, the toe vanished, and its mate showed briefly as the man turned slightly and stepped back a pace.

Stuck, Ki mused bitterly; he was not even going to be able to reach the top. It wasn't a simple matter of waiting out the sentry; sooner or later the sentry would happen to glance down and spot him, and perhaps sooner than that, the men from the camp would be arriving.

Ki thought it over for another moment, then wedged himself as securely as he could against the slope, and dug one of his *shuriken* out of his vest pocket. In a friendly, almost jaunty voice, he called up: *"Buenas tardes, Señor!* Do you have a match?"

"Eh?" A hatbrim appeared. Startled eyes peered down, blinking, tobacco-stained lips opening to gape, the barrel of a Sharps beginning to dip low, aiming toward Ki. Ki flicked his *shuriken* underhand, sending it whirring upward in a shallow curve. It sliced through the bridge of the sentry's nose, burying its razored tips at an angle by his left eye. The head dropped forward, the sentry's big body sliding over the rim, angling directly at Ki, gathering momentum as it plunged.

Sideways, into the slim nook to which his left hand clung, Ki pressed his limber body. The sentry's falling body brushed his shoulder, nearly ripping him loose. Shaken, frantically gripping his precarious hold, Ki heard the sentry strike the trail below with a sodden thud.

After taking a moment to regain his breath, Ki began to work his way upward as before. He reached the stone ledge, and with the remaining strength in his arms he shinnied himself up and over, to lie flat on his face, sucking in air with great, heaving gasps. Recovering, his exhausted body strengthened, he rose and picked up the sentry's rifle. It was a virtual blunderbuss, a Sharps "big fifty" buffalo gun, of the type potent enough to bag a target at eight hundred yards.

Ki now turned his back upon the deep crevice and

viewed the sharp pinnacles of rock that reared like sawteeth beyond. A narrow stretch of flat plateau intervened, flanking the canyon. He sprinted along it, finding where the trail connected and following it back toward the steps, the long gun crooked in his elbow. Ordinarily he disliked firearms, but the day had been far from ordinary, and the Sharps was the only long-range, stop-'em-in-their-tracks weapon they had.

In a few minutes Ki had crossed the level ridge and was loping down the steep incline. He didn't see Jessie or Evita—or any of the horses, for that matter—and he realized they must have hidden themselves when they'd heard somebody descending. He called out, identifying himself, and a moment later the women appeared from behind the large boulder. They were riding bareback, Evita leading the sentry's horse by its reins.

"The saddled one's for you," Evita said. "Hurry!"

"Don't argue," Jessie cut in wearily, when Ki began to protest. "She's stubborner than a cross-eyed ox. Besides, I hear riders."

Shrugging, Ki swung into leather and eased the sentry's pinto forward. They rode into the defile, and now Ki too could hear the pounding rhythm of hoofbeats in the distance. Nevertheless, when he came to the contorted corpse of the sentry, he reined in and dismounted.

"What are you up to?" Jessie snapped. "He's dead."

Evita shook her head. *"Que lástima—*what a pity."

"Yes," Ki said, hastily rummaging through the man's pockets and transferring handfuls of .50-caliber shells for the Sharps to his own vest pockets. Then he removed the sentry's cartridge belt and holstered

Remington .45, which he handed to Jessie before remounting. He smiled at Evita, saying softly, "You've got a heart, and it's a warmer one than you let on."

Evita flashed him a glare fit to scald, and jabbed the bay into a startled gallop. Jessie and Ki fell in quickly behind, following her through the dogleg shoulder and out the other side of the defile. Across the long open patch they sped, the sun blazing down on them; they had another hour, Jessie gauged, before it would start to set, an hour in which they'd be glaringly spotlit....

Evita led them into another canyon, then along a forested slope, their route gradually descending from the mountain heights, down from pinnacle rock and bouldery chasms. Above and behind them, they could hear the clatter of hooves against stone, the faint shouts of their pursuers breaching the shoulder and finding the sentry.

Down they continued, the trail now meandering across the heat-blasted foothills, through the ridge-flanking benches and brush-strewn arroyos. The western horizon was a thick crimson smear when they finally hit the broad desert tableland.

The noise of the chase was faint, but still audible. Evita pointed northwesterly, toward a faint rut that made an eroded and rubble-strewn path of sorts heading in the direction of Mosquero. "Quick, this way, before they get here and see us!"

"No," Ki said. "It's too flat out there. Maybe if this were night we could risk it, but even during dusk, they'd catch us with their rifles long before we could reach town."

Jessie sighed, knowing Ki was right. "Is there any

other way around to Mosquero, Evita? One that'd give us a little cover?"

"*Sí*. To the east, then north."

Jessie, having passed through that section on the train, recalled it as a landscape of rolling grass hills with oak and pinyon in the draws—poor but supportable cattle country, if you grazed enough of it. She asked, "That's private ranchland, isn't it?"

Evita nodded. "Mostly it belongs to Señor Polhaus, but some of it's owned by a herder named York. He, at least, doesn't hate *mexicanos*."

Jessica had never met Mr. York, knew nothing about the man. But the notion of going anywhere near August Polhaus, that bigoted Mexican-hater and budding politico, left a sour taste in her mouth. "How long will that way take, Evita?"

"Several hours more. But it's our only hope, *verdad?*"

It appeared that was so to Ki as well. He didn't care to lose the extra time involved, not when a whole trainload of national leaders depended on swift warning; nor did he care to trespass on Polhaus's property, not when the prejudiced rancher could have his crew out prowling around. Yet the risk of crossing the open flatland, of trying to outrun the pursuing Renegaders, was infinitely greater—and after all, he and Jessie and Evita had to stay alive, if De Baca's and Von Eismann's sabotage at Purgatory Gorge was to be stopped.

"East it is," he said grimly to Evita. "Let's ride!"

He dug his heels into the pinto's ribs. Jessie and Evita raked their horses' flanks, then bent low over the flowing manes. They veered due east, while the setting sun inflamed the distant peaks they were now facing, and cast fiery hues over the rumpled, craggy earth they were now crossing, and radiated brilliant pointers toward the Polhaus ranchland.

★

Chapter 7

They rode without speaking, alternately running their horses at full speed and slowing them to a trot to conserve flagging energy. Their course wandered according to the lay of the land, keeping to depressions and bare stone whenever possible, while skirting clumps of cactus and prickly pear, and avoiding sandy stretches that would raise dust and leave prints. Now and then they'd glance over their shoulders, judging by the hazy plumes behind them that their pursuers were falling farther back all the while.

That was a relief, but Jessie wasn't sure it was that much of a help. Assuming they could lose their pursuers, assuming they could cross Polhaus's spread without incident, assuming they could double back westward again without getting lost, assuming absolutely no delays, there was still no guarantee that they'd reach Mosquero in time to wire Deming, the last station at which the train could be halted.

Shortly, Jessie noticed that her claybank was blowing heavily, and she could see that Ki's and Evita's mounts were laboring as well. When they came to the end of a shallow gulch, she signaled for them to slow to a walk. Turning, she looked back again. The dust cloud was still there, coming steadily.

"They're still after us," Ki allowed grimly. "I wish

they'd get tired of it, and head back into the mountains."

"They will, eventually," Evita said. "They're too few to risk being spotted by Señor Polhaus's *vaqueros*. Even Señor York would not show mercy to Renegaders." She gave a tired smile. "But they won't catch us now."

"We may know that, but they don't seem to," Jessie murmured, shifting wearily on the bare back of her horse. "Evita, do you know where Victor Harrigan was taken?"

The girl shook her head, her mouth taut with bitterness. "Don Felipe told us little of his plans. Yet we followed him like sheep."

She fell silent after that, and simply stared out over the broad valley ahead. Jessie had the feeling that she was contemplating her father's murder, and how it symbolized De Baca's betrayal of the revolution and, ultimately, of Mexico itself. Ki was right about her, Jessica thought; Evita was fiery and tempestuous and full of the kind of heart some folks called "guts," but hers was a heart that also held tenderness, sorrow, and regret.

They walked their horses for a while, then prodded them into a canter. Like a stained rug spread carelessly, the valley before them was crinkled and creased, seamed by alkali sinks, scarred by eroding buttes, pocked by brush thickets and palo verde trees. No cows were in sight, yet undoubtedly they were now crossing someone's rangeland.

On the far side of the valley rose another section of broken and chopped bluffs. They struck across them, only to encounter another valley. The dust cloud on their backtrail appeared to be dissipating, which meant that either their pursuers had turned tail or had chosen a wrong track. To which Jessica murmured a grateful "Thank God."

By now they were slack with exhaustion, logy from thirst and hunger, and the two women were sore, their inner thighs chafed raw from riding bareback. Less cautious of pursuit now, they let their horses seek their own pace, while they followed the meandering course of yet another of the seemingly endless series of herdless valleys.

Along one slope, a couple of hundred yards above them, erosion had etched a slender shelf. It ran more or less parallel with the floor of the valley and, because of numerous rocky overhangs, was murky with shadow. They climbed to the shelf and jogged along it, more in search of relief from the withering hot sunset than seeking shelter from a trailing gang of killers. Ki's pinto nickered softly, the way a horse will when dry and scenting water. Ki was about to suggest that they try to locate the water, when a ragged volley of shots erupted.

They stopped sharply, startled. A second volley crackled, echoing from ahead on the other side of the slope. "Sounds like quite a crowd," Ki said, as the crazed outburst faded and died.

"What'll we do, go back around?" Evita asked nervously.

"Around who? Renegaders? Polhaus's crew, or maybe York's?"

"Good point, Ki," Jessie observed. "This pasture's getting mighty popular. It might be worthwhile to find out more, if only to learn where and how far we'll have to go to avoid trouble."

Evita followed reticently as they began picking a path up among the littered boulders, working quietly· toward a copse of trees growing along the brow of the slope.

When they crested the hill, they saw that the trees continued sparsely down its other side, ending at the edge of what the Mexicans called a *vallecito*, a small pocket valley. Its floor was mostly the typical summer drypan, straw stubble, and web of dry-wash gullies; but not far to their right was a low outcrop and a wide, shallow pool, around which sprouted bucknut, sage, and foot-high tufts of bluestem grass—among which lay three bodies, one of them twitching.

There was also a knot of four sombreroed horsemen, sitting their mounts next to the pool, while a fifth rider waded his horse back and forth. It was impossible to tell why the man was using his horse to stir up the water, but it appeared as though he was dragging something behind him by a length of rope.

Seeing the sombreros but not the faces they shaded, Jessie assumed that the men were De Baca's. "What're *they* doing *here?*" she asked.

"Shooting three men, for starters. What they're up to now, I can't tell." Ki dismounted, rifle in hand. "But I plan to stop it."

Sighing, Jessie slid down and told Evita, "Wait here."

"No, I want—"

"You're unarmed," Jessie interrupted her sternly. "We need you to hold the horses and to— Well, in case something happens, to carry word to the sheriff in Mosquero about the train."

Evita nodded grudgingly. *"De acuerdo.* My father died trying to stop that—that *bastardo,* Don Felipe. I can do no less."

Ki and Jessie threaded their way through the tangle of rocks, brush, and trees. Reaching the base of the slope, they eased over a cutbank onto the sandy floor of a dry wash, whose trench snaked more or less in the direction of the pool. They moved closer, hunching low, hearing the one rider splashing inexplicably in the water.

Then, pausing to raise their heads and gain their bearings, they saw that one of the other horsemen had cuffed back his sombrero to mop his brow. The man had a loose, ugly underlip that hung like a slice of raw flesh from his half-open mouth, and Jessie gasped, "He's not Mexican at all!"

Ki nodded in agreement, but recalling the man he'd knifed during the ambush at Mosquero's train depot, he cautioned, "But that doesn't mean he—and the rest of them—aren't Renegaders."

"Well, whoever they are, let's get this over with," Jessie whispered, ducking back down. "We don't have time to fool around."

Suddenly Ki's pinto nickered, louder and more impatiently this time. Almost instantly, the four horsemen drew weapons and triggered a barrage up into the tree shadows, while the fifth dropped whatever he'd been dragging and spurred his horse out of the pool.

Ki snarled an angry expletive. They'd lost the advantage of surprise, and Evita, weaponless, was under savage attack. Swiftly he straightened and let fly with the Sharps. Its report was deafening, and the face of

106

Ki's target disappeared, the body of the horseman lurching like a beheaded chicken before falling out of the saddle.

"One down," Ki muttered, chambering a fresh shell. "I'd have hit his heart, only he was wearing his shirt pocket too high."

"Doesn't matter where you hit with that cannon," Jessie retorted, ears ringing, as she fired the Remington .45. A second rider slumped, and his horse, whinnying in fright, bolted away.

The remaining three men lashed their mounts in separate directions, fanning out while bringing their guns to bear on the dry wash. Rifle and pistol fire reverberated through the fingerling valley, punctuated by the thunderous roar of the Sharps. A slug kicked grit into Jessica's face and she flinched instinctively. Above, to her left, a third rider toppled backward off his horse, falling heavily into the grass and lying unmoving, blood oozing from a neat hole drilled squarely between his lungs. Which left two more—

And those two were gone.

Jessie and Ki waited, listening intently, but not even the drum of retreating hoofbeats could be heard. Levering another shell into the breech of his rifle, Ki carefully peered over the bank. The evening-shadowed pool was deserted, except for two more corpses to add to the first pair, and the one feebly writhing body from before.

Feeling that something wasn't quite right, Ki cuddled the Sharps against his shoulder, alert for trickery. Abruptly, from where the dry wash ended back by the hillside, came the sound of running feet. Ki and Jessie pivoted, leveling their guns—almost firing.

"What the hell!" Ki snapped, recognizing Evita as she dashed toward them. Even Jessie was angry enough to curse. "Damn it!"

"But I heard . . . I was so worried!" Evita panted fretfully.

With equal suddenness, two men dove from the shriveled brush that mottled the rim of the dry wash. They'd been sneaking around in a flanking attack, that much was obvious to Ki—just as obvious as were the motives of the man with the ugly underlip, who, seeing an opportunity, pounced on Evita.

The other man landed a few feet in front, his gun-hand swiveling toward Jessie and Ki. He shot. But Jessie had fired a split second sooner. The narrow trough resounded to the twin discharges, the man's bullet spanging off the sunbaked dirt wall. Then he heeled to one side and sank to the dry-wash bed, weighted down with Jessica's .45 slug buried in his heart.

The one with the pendulous underlip, while struggling to get in an accurate shot with his pistol, shielded himself with Evita's twisting body. "Hold it!" he yelled. "You try'n plug me, the bitch gets it."

With that, he began to force Evita backward with him, jabbing the muzzle of his pistol into the nape of her neck. Helpless, Jessie and Ki eyed the two as they slowly moved out of the dry wash toward the first line of dark trees, in which the two men's horses would have been hidden. Evita stumbled, her hand twisted behind her in a painful armlock, her features pale, desperation in her eyes. The man faced the dry wash, only his taut, ugly face visible over her right shoulder.

"What a fuckup," the man snarled loudly. "But I

108

swear it, I do, whoever you bastards are—I'll blow her brains out if you try following!"

Indistinctly now, as the saddlehorses in among the trees began to mill restlessly, raising a dust cloud, they saw the man set the girl in one saddle, then mount the other horse. They galloped out in a great roil of dust, swung around the base of the hill, and disappeared.

"I'm going after her," Ki said, starting for his own horse.

"Very well, I suppose we must."

"Alone."

"You'll be riding blind, Ki."

"Jessie, one of us must go to Mosquero. You."

"Without Evita guiding, I don't know how to get there!"

Ki rubbed his forehead, trying to clear his fatigued mind. "Look, Polhaus's ranch house can't be too far, or too hard to find. Go there, and either get directions or have him relay our message. I'll take Evita's bay along for her to ride, and we'll meet you there later."

"I don't like it!" she called after him, as he started sprinting back up the hill. If he heard her, he didn't acknowledge, and was quickly lost in the trees as he scrambled up to the horses.

Irritably, Jessica climbed out of the dry wash. She stood for a moment listening to Ki descending the hill bareback on the bay, leading the pinto by its reins, then pounding off in the direction in which the fugitives had ridden. She was about to hasten back to her own claybank when she heard another noise—a soft moaning coming from the wounded man.

She couldn't simply leave him.

As much as she might have wished to, as much as she realized that time was of the essence, she couldn't abandon a stricken person. Urgency still uppermost in her mind, though, she approached him hurriedly.

It was obvious that he was one of the victims, not one of the raiders. His hat wasn't a sombrero, but a frayed old cavalry-style campaign hat, and the rest of his range garb was of the same worn, ill-fitting, hand-me-down variety. He was lying on his back, a tow-headed youth in his late teens. The problem was, he was suffering a man-sized wound; the upper right chest of his shirt was sodden with blood.

Jessie lifted him a little, and when she didn't feel any exit wound along his shoulder blade, she took a chance and tenderly peeled off his shirt. As she began wrapping it in a makeshift bandage around his chest, the youth chuckled and said, "You're just wastin' time."

"I've seen worse," she hedged. "Don't talk."

"Me? Never. That's why they call me Gabber. Anyhow, I wanna talk, lady. I ain't got no other way to thank you for tryin'."

"Skip the thanks, and tell me where Polhaus's ranch is."

"You don't know? You're not . . . ?" He slumped, shaking his head weakly. "'Course you ain't, else you wouldn't be patchin' me up." In an increasingly fragile voice, he gave Jessie directions, ending with, "But if I was you, I'd stay the hell an' gone away from his place."

"You need doctoring. I'll have someone sent out for you."

The boy tried to laugh; it came out a choking cough.

110

"Lady, the kinda help Polhaus'll send will help me plumb into my grave."

"I don't understand. Don't you work for Polhaus?"

"Hell, no. I ride for Mr. York. Fact is, that's what me an' Walsh an' Stubby were doin', riding Mr. York's range, when we got blasted."

"But I thought Polhaus owned this land."

"He'd like to, and he's been tryin' to buy it. 'Cept Mr. York, he don't like Mr. Polhaus's manner of doin' business, or all his spite-talk about Mexes. He also don't much like Mr. Polhaus's plans for expansion."

"Expansion?"

"Mr. York, he swears Mr. Polhaus fancies a vision of owning all the graze 'tween Mosquero an' the border. Building hisself a li'l empire, Mr. York says, and that's why Mr. Polhaus is getting into politics, too."

"So what you're saying is—"

"That's right, lady. The jiggers who shot us, they're some of Polhaus's crew. I knowed them by sight. An' if'n you want to know what they was up to, take a gander at the pool."

Jessie straightened and went to the water's edge. In the marshy shallows she spotted the outline of a feed sack, with a length of rope knotted tightly to one corner. Thinking that this must be what the rider had dropped, she waded in and retrieved it. The water around the sack was chalky white; its contents were half gone and dissolving rapidly, oozing more whiteness from the holes in the burlap. There was a stenciled likeness of a bull's head on its front, encircled by the words, BULA & SONS' PURE QUICKLIME.

"Careful, lady. You can get burned 'n poisoned."

"Evidently that was their idea," she replied, cautiously dragging the sack out into the grass. "This spring may never be any good again for watering livestock. You'll have to make tests."

He didn't respond.

"Gabber? You hear me?"

Silence.

Jessie hastened to him. He was stretched out limply, his left hand bent across his wound, his eyes staring sightlessly at the dusky sky.

"Bless you," she whispered, closing his eyes. "Rest quiet."

Moments later, Jessie was riding her claybank mare down from the copse of trees and off in the direction the youth had told her to take. The things he'd told her preyed on her mind—as did the crying shame of his death—and what he hadn't explicitly told her, she now began to extrapolate. The answers she came up with were brutal.

August Polhaus was greedy and vicious. Whether or not he was as much a bigot as he acted was immaterial; he was taking advantage of the Renegaders' incursions to do some private raiding of his own, ruining neighboring ranchers like York while blaming it all on the Mexicans. There was no telling how much of a liar and hypocrite he was; it was even conceivable to Jessie that Polhaus was in cahoots with De Baca to create a reign of terror, so that they could carve out their own private dictatorships on each side of the border.

The last was sheer speculation, Jessica admitted. The action at the pool showed Polhaus to be cruel and unscrupulous, but it didn't automatically link him to

112

that other megalomaniac, De Baca. As an unprincipled opportunist, Polhaus was much more liable to figure it would be to his political advantage to help save the train from destruction.

Yet whatever Polhaus was, Jessie wasn't about to trust him until she felt satisfied how he would jump. Like it or not, she was going to have to visit him. Ki expected to meet her at his ranch, and he had to be warned.

Whatever else Polhaus was, he'd proven to be a killer.

Chapter 8

Topping a shallow rise, Jessie halted her tired horse and sat resting. It had taken almost two hours to reach here, but now, finally, on the flat below lay Polhaus's ranch. Her first impression was that it was almost the size of Mosquero. It was hard to tell; the wood and adobe buildings blended with the increasingly night-darkened terrain.

The only points of contrast were the black silhouettes of the buildings, and the outlines of brush and trees fringing a creek that flowed nearby. Facing the creek was the two-story main house. Across a wide quadrangle were the bunkhouse and mess hall, both built barracks-style. Two barns, a storage silo, and a smithy's shed were along the sides, and across the creek, horses grazed in a large corral.

Lamplight spilled from the bunkhouse window, and more light filtered from behind a couple of curtained windows in the main house. Yet the yards appeared empty, the entire ranch deathly still in the budding moonlight. Its aura of desertion made one of Jessica's worries surface more strongly than ever. Maybe Polhaus wasn't here; maybe he was out with more of his crew, maybe—

Maybe she'd damn well better find out, she chastised herself, sliding down. The claybank mare seemed amiably disposed to stay put, so, leaving it to nibble grass in a nook between boulders, Jessie made her way to the flat, careful not to brush against brittle scrub or set loose gravel rolling. At the bottom, she paused in the shadow of a chokecherry tree, again spotting nothing, and not liking it.

Her uneasiness was sharpened when she thought she saw vague movement by the rear porch of the main house. Then a fat woman took shape, as she stepped out and tossed a dishpan of water into a garden patch. Some chickens began squawking in their coop next to the patch; they quieted after the woman went back inside the house.

Jessie waited a few more minutes. Feeling satisfied that the movement she'd glimpsed had been the woman—and only the woman—she darted across the open yard to the first shed. Using the splash of light from the house as a beacon to guide her, she advanced alongside the shed and over to the side of the house. Wending her way past obstacles, she eased toward the lighted windows, hearing now a low murmur of voices.

Eager to catch the conversation, Jessie slipped closer to the windows. Too close—she realized abruptly that she was standing so that she was framed in the light, and she dropped back from the window.

A man's voice snapped, "Come away from there, mister."

She pivoted, crouching to draw . . . then stopped and relaxed. A tall, angular man with a sandy mustache was approaching from the corner, his revolver leveled. "Smart. You'd never have made it," he said as he neared. Then, squinting, he blurted out, "Crap, it's a female!"

Jessie shrugged. At the same moment there was a shuffling of boots behind her, and glancing around, she saw the shadowed figures of two other men closing in. There was enough light to see the glint of their pistol barrels, and their toothy grins of anticipation.

The man with the sandy mustache stepped closer to Jessie, but paused when she turned to face him squarely. "Give it over," he told her.

Jessie eased her Remington .45 out of its holster and handed it to the man. He stuck it in his belt, then gestured with his revolver for her to follow him. She fell in step, the other two dogging a few paces behind. They filed around to the front, where she was hustled inside and along an elaborately decorated corridor to a sliding oak door. The man knocked once, politely, and slid open the door.

"You got a visitor, sir," he said, ushering Jessie in.

The room was opulent with velvet sofas, over-stuffed chairs, and large, heroic paintings of battle scenes on the paneled walls. From the middle of the ceiling hung a cast-frame, frosted-globe extension lamp of cannon ball proportions; beneath it was a massive wood pillar table, its surface inlaid with a checkerboard.

Two men were seated at the table, playing checkers. One was August Polhaus, dressed as Jessie had last seen him, his expression sour with acute annoyance as he said, "Well, if it ain't Miss Starbuck!"

The other man was Victor Harrigan. He had a rope tied around his wrists, and was still wearing Doc Scofield's bandage on his left leg, but otherwise nothing. Nary a stitch. Mortified, face reddening, he dropped his bound hands to cover his exposed groin, and opened his mouth to say something.

Jessie shook her head and Harrigan remained silent, while Polhaus shifted in his chair. "Where'd you run across her, Ike?"

"Snoopin' by them windows," the mustached man answered.

"It's all a mistake. I was passing and thought to visit, only you've got such a *big* house, and I got *so* turned about," Jessie protested coquettishly. "Why, what *have* I interrupted—strip checkers?"

Polhaus laughed harshly. "Mr. Harrigan's condition is merely to prevent his wandering. I'm sure something finer and nobler drew you here, Miss Starbuck, but whatever it is, it's a pity . . . for you."

"I declare, you're mystifying me."

"Stop acting the ninny, you're not fooling me one whit. Now that you're here, though, I might just be able to use you."

"How?"

"Two ransoms could be doubly effective, doubly lucrative."

Again Harrigan opened his mouth, this time starting to rise; again Jessie gestured to him to keep still, while she regarded Polhaus with eyes as hard as bottle glass. "Is that all you can think of, how to use people? How to use their fears, their griefs, their legitimate concerns to further your own selfish ends?"

Polhaus laughed. "We all use one another to get on top. That's how the jungle of life operates, and for proof, just see where it's gotten me and where it's landed you and Harrigan. Yes, and that's how Renegado plans to get on top, by using his ragamuffin believers to conquer Mexico; and that's how De Baca plans to get on top, by using Renegado."

117

"And how Von Eismann plans to use you and De Baca?"

"My, you have been a busy sneak, haven't you?"

"Just an educated guess. But don't you realize that crooks as cold-blooded as Von Eismann, and those who use *him,* can never be trusted to keep their word? That they'll use and eventually dump you, just as De Baca hopes to dump Renegado? You're not using, you're being used!"

"Another nice try, Miss Starbuck, but equally unpersuasive. I'm too powerful to be dumped, as you put it, and shortly I'll be even more powerful, when I become territorial governor." He glanced at Ike, saying, "Take her to the cellar," then flicked his eyes over Harrigan. "Take 'em both. I feel sorta tired of playing games."

"So do I," Jessie snapped, as she began drawing her hidden derringer from behind her belt buckle. Seeing her move sparked Harrigan into action, and straightening, he thrust against the table to send it toppling against Polhaus.

Yet even as Jessica drew, Ike seemed to sense the danger and leaped at her. And Polhaus, with quicker reflexes than one would have imagined, lunged upright and punched Harrigan in the face. A startled sound broke from Harrigan as the blow struck solidly, and he reeled back into his chair, while Ike caught Jessie at the wrist and trapped her derringer in a twisting grip.

The other two men were closing in, but they weren't needed. Polhaus dove around the table, cocking his fist for a second blow. Ike was in a bit more trouble. Jessie was clawing at his face with her left hand, her nails drawing blood down his cheek and slashing perilously close to his right eye. Cursing, Ike cracked her gun arm across the point of his knee, wrenched her derringer free, and flung her aside.

"Shit, what a spitfire!" he growled, daubing his cheek.

"Yeah, and with secret teeth." Crossing, Polhaus grabbed her derringer from Ike, then glared at Jessica. "All right, peel."

"Wh-what?"

"I don't relish no more surprises." His eyes were hot, his lips an angry gash. "So it's to the buff for you, Miss Starbuck."

Jessie drew a shuddering breath, staring about the room: at Harrigan slouching dazed in his chair, blood trickling from his bruised mouth; at the grinning Ike and the other two men, one gangly and pockmarked, the other burlier and balding, and both breathing heavily; then at Polhaus, scornful, aiming the derringer at her.

"Strip, Miss Starbuck. Or *be* stripped."

Jessie began to undress. She moved languidly, indifferently, purposely ignoring the effects she knew she was causing, as she slid out of her jacket and blouse, releasing her firm, quivering breasts. Unbuckling, then unbuttoning her jeans, she bent slightly to slide each pantleg and boot off. Her thin nainsook drawers slipped teasingly into the crevice of her buttocks from the pressure of her stooped position.

The drawers remained bunched in the hollows as she straightened. She untied the drawstring. She attempted to be nonchalant, consciously behaving as if she were in the privacy of her own bedroom as she began to roll down her drawers. Nevertheless, the men gaped pruriently while she slowly, slowly worked her drawers over her thighs and buttocks. They puddled on the floor around her feet, like a white flag of surrender.

She stepped from them, defiant. "Satisfied?"

"Not quite," Polhaus replied snidely, and tossing a short length of rope to the mustached man, he ordered, "Truss the bitch up, Ike."

Ike advanced, his tongue moistening his lips. Jessie tried twisting away in abhorrence, but his muscular hands promptly seized her, catching both of her wrists and wrestling her into submission. Then he stepped back, leering with the others as lamplight gleamed around the curves and hollows of her buttocks, breasts, and belly, throwing into relief her tied hands and naked flesh.

Ike said, "There, that oughta hold her."

"I got sump'n that'll hold her better," the balding man cracked, and the pockfaced man snickered, adding, "Hell, you'll hafta take turns, Will. Harrigan there, he's really in love."

A general guffaw greeted the remark. Harrigan didn't laugh, though; he was a hapless, vivid pink. Nor did Jessica appreciate the humor as, glancing at Harrigan, she saw that his hands, cupped over his crotch, failed to conceal all of his rigid erection.

She averted her face, embarrassed for him, but neither shocked nor insulted by what she knew to be an involuntary, natural reaction. No, the outrage she felt was at being forced to stand nude in front of these sadistic lechers—who themselves sported bulges in the groins of their pants—and rather than humiliation

120

and shame, her response was cold hatred and revulsion.

"Polhaus, I warn you," Jessie said with bitter ferocity, "you'd best kill me now, for I swear I'll kill you if you don't."

"In time, perhaps, I'll kill you. In time." Polhaus, reading her mask of feral loathing, sneered contemptuously and tossed her derringer on top of her pile of clothing. "Get rid of 'em, Ike."

Wincing from Ike's viselike grip on her arm, Jessie was marched out of the room. Behind her came Harrigan, gritting his teeth against the pain of his wounded leg, the two men roughly dragging him between them. The prisoners were prodded along another corridor toward the rear of the house, and were halted near the kitchen by a flight of steps down to a cellar.

Ike lit a bracket lantern, then ordered Jessie to go first. He grinned appreciatively as he watched the cheeks of her buttocks jiggling while she descended to a narrow, dark passageway. From there the procession filed through a repugnant tunnel, boots and bare feet squelching against the clammy flagstones, until they came to a hollowed-out chamber, a cul-de-sac not much wider than the tunnel itself.

Jessie and Harrigan were thrust inside, where, sprawling, they were left plunged in darkness as the heavy wooden door of the chamber was slammed behind them and a heavy latch bolt was thrown. Then came the sound of retreating boots.

Jessie sat up and gazed about frantically, but was unable to discern anything in the gloom. She tugged futilely at her ropes, and her movements seemed to rouse Harrigan. Worming his way across the floor,

121

he touched her thigh—and drew his hand back as if burned.

"Sorry, Jessie."

"There isn't time for modesty, Victor. Quick, untie me."

"I'll try."

It proved difficult; Harrigan's own hands were so tightly bound that he couldn't manipulate his fingers very easily. Frustrated, he bent forward and caught a stubborn loop in his teeth. His head rubbed against her breasts as he gnawed at the loop, his hair brushing her sensitive nipples. Jessie sensed a slight tremor of response to his inadvertent caress, but choked it down, concentrating instead on helping him. He kept working at her knots with fingers and teeth, unconsciously stroking her over and over... until despite herself, Jessie moaned softly as she sensed small erotic throbs tingling up between her legs.

"What's wrong? Did I hurt you?"

"Far from it, Victor. Keep working, I feel them loosening."

And me with them, she thought, pressing her thighs firmly together to try to contain the perverse sensations he was accidentally producing in her. Oblivious, Harrigan continued wrenching and plucking on her ropes, until finally they unraveled and fell off her wrists.

"Good," she sighed. "Now you."

She set to work. Her fingers were bleeding when she somewhat reluctantly concluded that she'd have to use her teeth to draw the knots. She leaned forward, biting, yanking, her breasts swaying tauntingly against his trapped hands... and worse, at one point one of her hands brushed against the velvety tip of his manhood, swelling from his groin. Reflexively she ground her buttocks against the cold floor while she slaved on. At last the bonds dropped free, and Harrigan stretched his aching arms to revive circulation.

Jessie rose unsteadily to her feet. "Let's explore this place and see if there's any way out," she suggested. "Can you walk?"

"If I can't," Harrigan replied, "I'll crawl."

He hobbled, as together they pawed like blind people through the room. They found a chair and a broken table, some tins and buckets, and a great many flour sacks piled haphazardly in one corner; but they only discovered the one door, no windows, no other exit. Dejectedly they sat down on the flour sacks.

"No way," Jessie said glumly.

"Doesn't look like it," Harrigan agreed. "If we had a gun, we might hold 'em up when they came in again. Wait a minute..." Harrigan scrambled over to the broken table, which he set about breaking even more. He came back with two of its legs, one of which he handed to Jessie. "Okay?"

Jessie tapped her makeshift club against her other hand. "Okay."

Then they settled down to painful waiting—for what, they did not know. The monotony was broken at first only by desultory conversation. Jessie asked, "What'd Polhaus mean by 'ransom'?"

"It's all a ploy. Supposedly it's to appear that the Renegaders are holding me hostage, forcing our government to negotiate, while Polhaus goes ranting and raving about, rattling his sword, so to speak."

"I see. If you'd simply been killed, there'd have been an uproar, a funeral, and everything would've died down. This way, Polhaus uses you to keep tension boiling, as your kidnapping grinds on."

"And now you too, Jessica."

She shook her head, thinking of Von Eismann. "I doubt it."

"Well, I sure don't know anything. This is all I've managed to gather from Polhaus and that man at the mine. I woke up in that place with the goddamnedest headache."

"You were drugged by the hotel clerk," Jessie explained. "We traced you to the mine, but by then, they'd already moved you on."

"How'd you know I was here?"

"I didn't. Chalk it up to luck."

"Some luck," Harrigan groused.

"Oh, it could be worse."

"How?"

"I could be locked in here alone."

He chuckled nervously and placed his hand lightly, affectionately on her leg. "Thanks. You're a pretty prime filly to be with, too."

"You're not bad yourself." She leaned back on the flour sacks, and reached out a hand to run her fingertips down his chest and belly. When she reached his groin, she said teasingly, "Why, Victor, I believe you're up to something."

He groaned, then pulled her to him. She curled an arm around and snuggled against him as he pressed his lips tightly against hers. The kiss was long. He ended it gradually. She protested in her throat, feeling squirmy inside.

He whispered, "Are you . . . willing? Now, in here, like this?"

"Let's just say I'm in the nude for love."

Goaded by passion, Harrigan kissed her again, harder. Jessie was surprisingly soft and supple, and her body was glued to his as though it belonged there. She pressed her thigh against his crotch as he ground his mouth harshly into hers, her sensual movements sending chills up the length of his spine.

He broke their fevered embrace, rising slightly to hover above her, his hands prowling over her breasts and nipples. She squirmed, sighing, his touches igniting her... and then shivered as Harrigan dipped his head down to her trembling belly and tongued her navel. She whimpered, tangling her fingers in his hair while his tongue moved farther down and thrust deep, teasing her sensitive loins and drinking from her inner flesh. Her thighs clenched spasmodically around his laving tongue and nibbling lips, tendrils of excitement rippling up inside her.

He eased his tongue inside at the bottom of her cleft and drew it up... up toward her tingling clitoris. Jessie held her breath, exhaling sharply at the delicious contact. Harrigan pressed his mouth closer and reached up with both hands to play with her breasts, his mouth becoming a hungry, hot invader, spearing her with his tongue, nipping tenderly with his lips and teeth. Jessie moaned. A minute... two minutes... her belly rippled. She began to pant explosively. Her hips curved up, her groin grinding against his face with pulsating tension....

And Jessie climaxed. She wailed, "Ohh, Lord..." and twisted in the clutch of her sweet agony, writhing and throbbing and refusing to break with the mouth that played like summer lightning against her moist

125

pink flesh. She shuddered and relaxed . . . or *tried* to relax, as Harrigan continued and she felt herself building to another crest. "That's enough . . . I'm ready . . . ready for you . . ."

Harrigan eased up alongside her. "Climb on."

Jessie turned over on her hands and knees, squatting to straddle his hips, feeling his hot length burning against her crotch. She reached under with her right hand and grasped him, positioning his thick crown between her moist nether lips, her loins absorbing the girth of his spearing shaft as she lowered herself slowly yet eagerly upon it.

She fastened her mouth on his and played moaning, electrifying tongue-games with him. Her stiffened nipples and aching breasts flattened against his hairy chest while she impaled herself completely, until the last inch of him was driven, throbbing, up inside her belly.

He asked, "Too much? Hurt?"

"Yes . . . *no!*" Jessie wriggled on him and felt his swollen bulk stir and shift in her. She began sliding on him, slowly at first, then with increasing enthusiasm as the erotic sensations intensified. Soon she was rearing high until his erection was almost totally exposed, then plunging down to enclose him fully, gasping, trembling as the shaft surged into her depths like a fleshy bludgeon, igniting her sensitive passage, searing her womb.

They clutched each other, kissing, panting, working rhythmically for the mutual release of pleasure they both felt building. Jessie's pounding thighs matched Harrigan's pumping upthrusts, her tender channel squeezing, squeezing, while he rammed deeper, more swiftly, pummeling her with spiraling ecstasy.

Then Jessie felt his rutting manhood grow even larger in its pre-orgasmic surge, saw his eyes sparkle with lust, and felt his tension and quickening motions. Harrigan's final, bruising thrusts triggered her again. She whimpered, sobbing, as her second climax overwhelmed her.

"Ohhh . . . Ohhh . . . !"

She arched and plunged madly, ground herself against him, dug her fingers into his arms, cried and half strangled, her face, neck, and breasts flushed with blood. She felt Harrigan come, felt him vibrant and huge within her as he groaned, his body stiffening, his hot juices jetting deep into her belly. . . .

They fell limp. Jessie lay on him and crooned, "That was good . . . so good . . ." He held her in his arms and drew in lungfuls of air, then tenderly kissed her face and nipples, still pumping slowly, with a dwindling erection barely firm enough to permit motion.

Gradually, Jessie became aware of the sweet ache in her stretched loins, the fatigue in her sore legs and back. She sighed, thinking about asking him to stop . . . but then she felt his meaty shaft regaining hardness and length.

"God . . ." she murmured, shivering. She was enervated, drained, lethargic, yet as Harrigan continued his gentle thrusting, she found that her loins were responding in kind.

"Lord, you're insatiable," she panted.

"So're you."

She began undulating responsively, gliding along

the length of his reviving shaft, her clitoris tingling with each pushing impact against his hard pubic bone. She closed her eyes, feeling her passions rekindling inside her—

Then raucous voices sounded outside in the tunnel.

The sensual spell shattered, she jerked up and jack-knifed off Harrigan's loins. Equally startled, Harrigan twisted, pivoting into a crouch, groping for the table legs and handing one to Jessica.

"Of all the damn times," he muttered, as they darted across to the door. Jessie, flashing him a taunting smile, whispered, "Be thankful. A couple of minutes earlier, we'd never have heard them."

". . . not have another chance," one man was say-ing—one of the two who'd sided Ike. "Be a shame to waste her."

"Be a stink if'n she blabs," the other cautioned.

"She won't, less'n she wants her throat slit. Hell, she'll prob'ly like a nice pokin', Will. Settle her right down, I betcha."

The key grated in the lock, and Jessie flattened herself behind the door as it squeaked open. Then, as light from the bracket lantern beamed into the chamber, the two gunhands eased inside. Instantly, Jessie shoved the door closed, and each of the intruders, thinking the other had shut it, gave it no heed.

The moment the door latched, Harrigan swung his table leg. It connected with a dull thud; simultaneously there came the noises of a heavy body falling, and of a lantern clattering. The light snuffed out.

"Will?" The other man began groping. *"Will!"*

The silence was intense, and each second seemed an age. Then Jessie felt a hand touch her arm, and smelled fetid breath she knew wasn't Harrigan's. Immediately she struck out with her table leg, and felt it connect with a meaty smack. There was a groan, and a figure hinged and crumpled sideways to the floor. She stood for a moment, savoring a certain satisfaction, then knelt and began stripping the man.

"Guns and clothes," she said. "What more could we ask for?"

"About ten more minutes alone," Harrigan grumped good-naturedly.

Jessie laughed. "Later, Victor, I promise . . ."

Dressing hastily in pants and shirts, they grabbed the men's revolvers and slipped outside, locking the chamber door behind them. Barefoot, they padded back through the dark tunnel, feeling the walls carefully with their hands, and crept up the stairs to the main floor.

The corridor was empty and dim, but there was sufficient light for them to see how ill-fitting their clothes were. Jessie's hung on her like a baggy clown suit, while Harrigan's looked as though he'd outgrown them in grade school.

"You'd be better off in these," Jessie commented, "and I'd be better off in my own, if I can find them. C'mon, let's try."

"T'hell with our clothes, let's just get away from this place," Harrigan insisted, gesturing toward the rear of the corridor. Beyond lay a kitchen, a portion of its large cast-iron stove visible in the doorway; obviously it connected directly with the backyard.

He turned toward the kitchen—then stopped, hearing a clatter of dishes and the trill of an unseen woman singing to herself. He shrugged. "Okay, we'll try. We

129

have to go the front way, anyhow."

Breathlessly they sprinted up the corridor, fearing that their footfalls might be audible. They paused by the double doors of the room in which Jessica had stripped naked; the doors were slightly ajar, and peering in cautiously, Jessie saw that nobody was there now.

Opening the doors wider, they slid inside the room. While Harrigan silently closed the doors, Jessie swiftly changed into her own clothes, which were where she'd left them, piled on the floor. She put on her boots and tucked her derringer behind her belt buckle, eyeing Harrigan appreciatively as he quickly peeled off his duds and traded them for the larger-sized pants and shirt she'd been wearing.

"Ready?" she asked.

"Ready," he replied.

They went to the doors and gently reopened them.

And found themselves face to face with August Polhaus.

"You were right, Ike." Polhaus was pointing a Colt .45 right at Jessica's breast. "I dunno how they managed it, but when you said you thought you heard them in here, you were damn well right."

The mustached *segundo* slipped in alongside his boss, his own revolver covering Harrigan. "Okay," he said, "Shuck those guns into the hall."

Jessie and Harrigan obeyed reluctantly, knowing they'd be shot before they could level their weapons. They tossed their pistols past the men, hearing them land far out of reach in the corridor.

Harrigan grinned ruefully. "Well, down to the cellar again."

130

But disdainful hatred was an overbearing force welling up inside Polhaus, and his intent to kill them was clear in his expression. "You'll be going deeper," he snarled. "Six feet deeper, into a grave."

Trapped! Jessica thought, watching Polhaus's finger closing on the trigger. . . .

Chapter 9

Earlier, while Jessie had been riding to Polhaus's ranch house, Ki had been doggedly tracking Evita and the killer.

From the start, Ki hoped the man would dump her as unneeded baggage along his way. He hoped this not only because, obviously, the sooner Evita was safe the better, but also because he realized almost immediately that trailing them would become increasingly difficult. At first it had been relatively easy; they'd only a limited head start, and their horses flung enough dust for him to trace them readily through a succession of interconnecting valleys and canyons. But their horses were fresher, and with time their lead grew considerably. And also with time came deepening shadows, until eventually even their dust cloud was lost in hazy purple dusk.

At last Ki was left with nothing to go on except the vaguely straight course the pair appeared to be taking. He followed in that direction, boring farther across the broken range land. Shortly he chanced upon a wide patch of loose sand, and halting, he swung down and struck a match, then began a close scrutiny of the surface.

It took a while, but Ki finally located a few distinct, freshly indented prints of shod hooves. Two other riders had recently passed through the patch, and at a gallop, judging by the marks' depth and spread.

Heartened, Ki remounted and renewed the chase. The odds were greatly against him, he knew, what with the killer outdistancing him and leaving precious little sign for night hunting, and evidently being familiar with the country, while Ki was not. But when the chips were down, Evita had risked her life for him and Jessie, and she still might prove to be an important help in stopping De Baca and Von Eismann. Ki would not—could not—abandon her without making every effort.

A ravine opened into a notch in the next low ridge, and taking it, Ki arrived at the soggy edge of another natural pool. It was smaller than the previous one, hardly more than a puddling mudhole fed by the seepage of some underground spring. Beyond lay sagebrush and a dark line that looked like shrubbery flanking a thin creekbed.

Ki checked the bay, stepping down again and allowing it and the pinto to lap the silty water. He cupped his hands and wet his mouth, then lit more matches to look around. The spongy earth was a morass of animal prints, but after surveying them, Ki thought he found some to match those he'd seen in the sandy patch.

The pinto and the bay were tuckered out. To rest them and to loosen his own stiff muscles, Ki led them for a while, walking the curves of the creek as it meandered through the ravine. He mounted again as the stars began to glimmer overhead. Riding blind, he allowed the bay to set the pace as the ravine funneled toward another ridge. A skittish breeze soughed through stalks of ocotillo; a nighthawk swooped to grasp a squeaking rodent. Ki continued, angling up out of the ravine and along the rubbled spine of the ridge, then paused on a hogback, slumping in his saddle, depressed and frustrated.

The slender crescent of moon emerged from behind banked clouds, gauzily illuminating the terrain below. A spark winked against its feeble glow. Ki strained his eyes, peering into the darkness. More clouds sifted in front of the moon, allowing Ki to discern the bright speck as the flames of a campfire in the near distance. Throwing off his lassitude, Ki started riding toward it, dipping down to the cratered rim of a dish-shaped valley, where he dismounted, not trusting the pinto not to nicker this time.

Set in a depression by a boxlike hill, the campfire was still too dwarfed by distance for Ki to make out details. He hooked the pinto's reins in an outthrusting root, and started forward afoot, moving as fast as caution permitted for the better part of a mile.

He approached the fire through a pinyon-thick draw, finally crouching to gauge the scene revealed by its flickering light: the ash-circle of a cooked meal; twelve saddled horses in a remuda; eight men lounging about, one of whom Ki recognized as the ugly-lipped killer. Beyond, near a massive fragment of stone, were three more men, standing and drinking from a leather water bucket, although Ki doubted that it held water right then. At the base of the rock, he thought he glimpsed a slim leg and the lower part of a dress. *Evita!* Sliding out of the draw, Ki snaked around toward her along a scrub-covered slope, overhearing conversation from the eight men grouped at the fire.

". . . Shouldn't have come here, Quincy."

The killer retorted, "Where'n hell else could I go?"

"Leastwise with the gal. Now she's seen us."

134

"Yeah, Quincy, and what about them other two seein' you?"

"It's a fuckup, okay, but I didn't do the fuckin' up!"

"Nobody's sayin' you did, Quincy. You an' your bunch got hit by surprise, is all, an' it coulda happened to any of us. 'Cept it didn't."

"It affects all of us, though. What now?"

"Tell the boss. He's gotta be told."

"He'll throw a conniption, and we still have more work to do."

"Okay, we won't. But we gotta get rid of them bodies."

The man with the water bucket leered drunkenly. "Speakin' of bodies, gents, what'll we do with this here gal?"

"Who cares?"

"Do whatcha want to, only make it snappy, Moe. We gotta break this up and get to ridin', if'n we're gonna get all done tonight."

"Hey, I bet she'd go for a drink," the second of the three men chortled, red eyes agleam in his dark, hatchet face.

"Hot damn, Sloan, a fine idea," the third rasped; heavy and brutish, he grabbed the bucket from Moe. "Us first, though."

Listening to the sounds of husky swallowing, Ki eased into a position where he could see Evita. She was sitting motionless on the ground next to the rock, the loop of a lasso around her neck, the rope attached to a wooden stake as though she were a pet on a leash.

"The hot tamale looks a touch peaked at that, fellers," the third man said, strutting over with the other

135

two, sloshing the bucket in crude invitation. "In sore need of a drink, in fact, I betcha."

"Bastardo," she cursed him, her back ramrod-straight.

"Do you dandy, gal," Sloan chuckled, hovering closer. "C'mon, you know stubborn missies can get hurt something fierce."

Savagely, he twisted his hand in her hair, pulled her head back, and thrust the lip of the bucket against her mouth. She clenched her teeth tightly, but the third man pressed harder, forcing her to accept the bucket rim between her lips. The rancid booze ran from the corners of her mouth and riveted down her neck.

Ki kept slithering nearer on his belly. His eyes flicked from the three men mauling Evita to the eight others lounging indifferently ten, maybe twelve yards away, then back to the three, while Moe laughed, still holding Evita tightly. "She-it, she's a true guzzler!"

"Here, take the bucket," the third man said to Sloan. "I'm gonna up that dress o' hers and climb into her saddle!"

"Aw, Luke, you always go first for everythin'."

"Yeah, Moe? Well, you got a better notion?"

"Why don't we cut cards?" Sloan suggested, grinning slyly. "High card rides her first, and the next highest follows."

The third man, Luke, glanced down at Evita, who glared back with seething contempt. Apparently the idea of further debasing this proud Mexican beauty appealed to his sadistic impulses, for Ki heard him say, "Fair 'nuff, fellers. Moe, get my cards outa my bag."

Moe sprinted for the remuda, and began pawing around in one of the mounts' saddlebags. Ki, moving scarcely an inch at a time, slipped around the base of the rock with his body flat to the ground. Finally he was able to see, not two feet from him, the curve of Evita's figure, outlined proudly and defiantly against the night.

Moe returned with a deck of greasy playing cards. Luke shuffled and handed the deck to Sloan, who cut a ten of diamonds. Moe turned over a seven of spades. Luke riffled the deck and drew the queen of clubs.

Ki's soft rustling made Evita glance his way. She didn't gasp or look startled; she smiled as though she'd been expecting him.

Ki wished there were more to smile about. True, at this close range it'd be a cinch to kill the men. Three *shuriken* or throwing daggers would drop them before they could reach their weapons, much less the campfire . . . but not before one of them might cry out. He'd have to silence them swiftly and surely.

"Hold 'er steady, fellers," Luke crowed as he began to unbutton his pants. "This here winner's about to rake in his prize."

From a sheath at the waistband of his trousers, Ki whipped out his *tanto,* a very short, delicately curved sword—no bigger than a knife, really—single-edged and razor-sharp. Among his other skills, he was trained in *iai,* the art of drawing the sword, the central precept of which was that the drawing of the sword, the cut, and the resheathing of the blade were a single motion. . . .

The closest man, Sloan, was leaning over Evita, and he never even saw Ki as the samurai brought the *tanto's* edge across the base of his neck, passing it between the vertebrae, slicing his spinal cord and bringing his misspent life to an end without so much as a whimper.

Even before Sloan's chin nodded forward against his chest, Ki was swiveling, continuing the tantò's arc to catch Moe, while lashing out with his slippered foot at Luke. Luke was on his knees between Evita's spread legs, and he was flung swiftly back by Ki's smashing heel kick to his throat and lower jaw. His jaw shattered and his larynx ruptured, Luke's call for help died stillborn. Moe had his mouth wide to yell, but could not because his windpipe was severed, along with his jugular veins, which fountained blood as he toppled over.

Again Ki pivoted, peripherally glimpsing Luke clawing for his revolver. Gasping, wheezing, doubled over in pain, Luke was driven by a mute fury that overcame his agony. But now he was vulnerable, no longer protected by his proximity to Evita, and Ki executed a forward somersault, rising in close and sliding his *tanto* into Luke's belly, gutting the man up through his chest cavity.

Withdrawing his knife, Ki quickly wiped its blade clean on Luke's shirt, as the gunman collapsed in a gory heap. Ki slashed the lasso rope, and while replacing his knife in his scabbard, he grabbed Evita by the hand and whipped her around behind the rock. Staggering, she rolled into his arms, murmuring, "I knew you'd find me, *mi malo matón.*"

"Well, I didn't," he responded gruffly, breaking her embrace. "And we've got a long way to go before we're safely out of here."

"D'you have a gun I can use? Where's that big rifle?"

"The Sharps is back with our horses," he told her.

"Let me grab one of their—"

"No, you're not setting foot out there! Come on!"

Moving very softly, testing each step for noise, they crept through the fringe of brush, covering the slope's last twenty yards on their stomachs. Dropping into the draw, Ki glanced back at the fire.

"I just hope they don't catch on for a while," he said.

And he'd no sooner said it than all hell broke loose. . . .

—"Luke, Moe? Hey, over there, why're you all so quiet?"

—"Jesus Christ, a massa-cree!"

—"The gal's gone, too!"

—"Injunned 'em somehow, and took off!"

—"Spread out, fellers! She can't've gone far!"

Ki swore, ducking with Evita along the draw. Behind them was utter chaos—shouts, the whinnying of horses, the uneven rattle of gunfire. . . .

—"There she is! I seen her!"

—"Who's that with her?"

Now slugs began snapping around Ki and Evita as the gunmen started to get their range. Lead plowed into the dirt at their feet, and spanged off the rocks protruding from the sides of the draw. As the fugitives ran past a place where the wall of the draw had crumbled, Ki grabbed Evita and pulled her along with him, scrambling up the pile of loose rock and into the flanking undergrowth.

—"Which way'd they go?"

—"In them bushes someplace!"

The eight pursuing gunmen riddled the underbrush with gunfire. The darkness was alive with the snap and whine of bullets. Rugged rocks and spurs loomed closer ahead; searching desperately, Ki spied the dark mouth of a narrow canyon. It lay in the opposite direction from their horses, and might prove to be a box, trapping them. Yet its stone walls loomed high, offering shelter that the draw and the rolling valley behind them could not.

Ki glanced back. The riders were trying to cut them off before they could reach the refuge of rocks. Stuttering volleys of lead chased after them as they plunged into the canyon. It made a turn, then another, and the slopes grew steeper. They saw a slim gully off to one side and darted into its narrow mouth, then twisted up into the rocks. Knowing it would be rank folly to try hiding at this point, they continued climbing the steep grade. But before they could clear the crest, the riders sent a heavy barrage winging their way.

They plunged over the rim, dropping behind a pile of loose rock as the fusillade sang around them. Immediately, Ki began pushing the rocks free, and Evita joined him.

Then, peering out over the remaining rubble, they saw the riders wrenching their horses to avoid the tumbling rocks and boulders. The horses shied, skewing and fishtailing, and bucked back from the slope. The ugly-lipped killer, Quincy, had one foot on the ground and the other lodged in his stirrup, in the process of either stepping in or out of his saddle. The avalanche spooked his horse, and jerking the reins out of his hands, it started dragging Quincy by his hooked boot across the canyon floor. Some of the other men dashed after him. Their loud swearing was imaginative and fulsome.

Ki and Evita hastened on into the wild fastness of the hills, moving in a wide sweep that they hoped would eventually bring them back around to the valley where their horses were waiting. They knew the riders would soon be on the prod again; there was nothing like bruised pride to foster dedication to the hunt. But Ki was determined not to make it easy for them, and he made sure to avoid open ground and skylines, clinging instead to rock and brush. Especially brush. And shortly, as they wound their way lower along the jagged slopes, the brush grew heavy with briars and thorny weeds.

The sound of crashing horses came to them from their right, toward the valley. They dove into the briar thickets as the horses trampled nearer, the riders peppering shadows with enraged abandon.

Ki and Evita pressed on through the stinging thorns and nettles. Then, abruptly, Evita gave a startled but muffled cry, and Ki saw her fall into a steep gully. He dove after her, landing hard, while above and behind them, the horses were balking chaotically at entering the briars. The men beat them around, the turmoil masking Ki and Evita's crawl up the opposite bank. Ki forged on through the switching weeds, Evita a wisp of gray ahead of him in the darkness. They came to a small, dusty clearing, the hardpan too dry to sustain even the meagerest of thistles.

"I have to rest," Evita gasped, and slumped to the ground. Ki sagged alongside her, and they lay silent, hearts pounding, lungs straining for air, listening to

141

the riders fade in the wrong direction.

"I think we shook them," Ki panted. "For a while."

"Long enough for us to get to our horses?"

"That's not the problem." Ki sat up, flexing his shoulders and chest. "The men are between us and our horses, that's the problem."

Evita sighed, staring at him. "So what do we do?"

He smiled wryly at her tattered *camisa*, smudged face, and tousled hair. He knew he must look as dirty and unkempt as she did. "We stay, for a while."

She snuggled closer. "I'm frightened," she whispered, and a shiver rippled through her that wasn't from cold. Ki placed an arm around and patted her shoulder to comfort her. He conjured up things to say that might encourage her, but she kissed him before he could open his mouth.

It was an affectionate kiss at first, lazy and teasing. Then it changed, and a smoldering passion seemed to take fire in her. She pressed against Ki, squirming and rubbing, her mouth like a bitter fruit that would give a man pain when he tasted it. She broke their embrace as abruptly as she'd begun it, and cuddled closer. "Why not, while we're staying?" she purred, grabbing for Ki's shirt and tugging.

Ki felt that he needed Evita like he needed a bad case of poison ivy. After the exhausting day he'd just put in, thanks mostly to Evita's seduction last night, he was hardly in any condition to promote a great, lathering romp, but he guessed that was what made men different from women. When a woman's ready, a man will somehow rise to the occasion.

He reached for her and got a handful of the thin *camisa*. He tugged; why not? She wanted him, and they were staying a while.

Ki pulled her *camisa* over her head, then Evita helped him out of his clothing. She crushed her naked body to his, kissing him with hot, moist urgency, first his lips, then the hollow of his neck, then lower to taunt his nipples. She slipped wetly along his abdomen, feeling its satiny skin ripple under her teasings. Then still lower, her lips probing and exploring as she heard Ki moan with swelling pleasure.

Evita gave a whimpering cry and leaned over to quickly taste his rampant erection. She licked the sensitive underside of the glans. She widened her mouth to absorb its thick crown, then ovaled her lips tightly around the corona, and began dipping her head up and down. She worked her tongue. She felt Ki stiffen harder and grow. She purred and slowed her action to a tantalizing, sensuous pumping that drew gasps from Ki and caused his hips to rotate against her.

She raised her head, licking her lips. "Do it," she mewed, and rolled over on her hands and knees. "The ground's too rough for my back and bottom, Ki, but do it to me . . . do it as good as you did last night . . ."

Ki positioned himself directly behind her, running his hands over the smooth cheeks of her soft buttocks. He could feel them quivering expectantly under his touch, and then he heard her moan as his aching shaft made electric contact with the tender lips of her upraised cleft. He felt her hand as she reached back under her body, her fingers urgently enfolding his girth, moving him up and down for a moment, parting her young flesh and guiding him gently forward.

"Ahhh," she sighed breathlessly, seeming to swallow the whole of him inside her as she slid back, impaling herself. Ki clasped his hands tightly around her wasplike waist, gripping her while he began to

143

stroke into her, his loins flattening her buttocks with each sawing thrust he drove into her gripping channel.

Leaning forward, Ki shifted one hand to knead her jiggling breast, toying harshly with her nipple, while she arched up and back like a bucking bronco. Her right hand again slid under her body, this time to caress Ki's scrotum, massaging him with the lightest of touches.

Tensing, he felt the squeeze of her loins pulling at his manhood, and he plunged faster, deeper, penetrating her with all his strength. And her passage kept squeezing, squeezing, hoarse moans keening from her slackened mouth. The squeezing became unbearable until, bursting, Ki came in a great gush.

Evita's clenching hips worked and sucked as if his hot seed were an invigorating tonic. Then, with a sigh of satiation, Evita slithered forward, releasing Ki's deflating erection, her inner thighs wet and glistening in the dim moonlight. Ki just hunched there, feeling vanquished.

An hour later they hiked, stiff-legged, to their horses. Once they heard the distant sounds of horses and men's voices, but never actually saw anyone, and reached the horses without incident.

Guided by Evita, they set off at a tangent directly for Polhaus's ranch, angling across rolling graze and barren range. Seemingly endless ground passed under their horses' rhythmic hooves, until Ki, yawning, noticed a golden glow rimming the hills ahead of them.

"It's taking longer than I thought. The sun's rising."

Evita looked. Then, rubbing her eyes, she looked again. "Ki, that's not the sun. It's a fire, and from its direction, it looks like it's Polhaus's ranch."

Ki straightened. "Jessie!"

They goaded their mounts to a gallop and at last they came to the edge of a gently rolling flat.

Polhaus's ranch house was a flaming pyre, billowing flame and smoke, and spreading the ghastly incandescence that Ki had spied from afar.

"Jessie's in there!" he cried.

"She can't be in there, Ki, not now!"

Anxiously they studied the ranch grounds. They spotted a number of hands from the bunkhouse milling about dazed and bewildered by the catastrophe; and in the vague reflection from the burning house, they glimpsed a couple of shadowy figures racing toward the corralled horses across the nearby creek. Then, faintly, above the roaring of the blaze, Ki thought he detected the drumming of hooves. Swinging about and squinting behind him, he perceived a turgid dust ball with eight black specks in it—the riders who'd been pursuing them were forging out of a trough between the distant hills, summoned by the glare of the fire.

Chapter 10

Trapped—

And with nothing to lose, Jessie realized, as Polhaus began squeezing the trigger. At the final instant she flung herself to the floor, whipping out her derringer while she dropped, twisting.

Ike shifted, distracted by her unexpected move. Harrigan used that split second of indecision to shoulder into him, and Ike lurched against Polhaus just as he shot. The blast seemed to rock the room, the .45 bullet skimming past Jessie's head, making her wince as she pivoted, crouching, and fired the derringer. It punched a .38 slug diagonally up through Ike's head.

The *segundo* stumbled sideways, his face an eruption of red. Again Polhaus was bumped, as Ike slumped against him while collapsing in the doorway. Before Polhaus could bring his pistol to bear, Harrigan slammed squarely into him, grabbing the barrel and trying to wrench the pistol out of Polhaus's grip.

A second shot discharged, and the large frosted globe of the extension lamp shattered, its bottom falling out, most of the reservoir of kerosene cascading onto the pillar table below. But some oil spattered and pooled, licked by a blue flame.

Harrigan drove his other hand in a fist to Polhaus's nose. His wounded leg buckled under the pressure of his thrust, and he missed, staggering off balance. Polhaus leaped aside, catlike, aiming his pistol. Jessie launched herself from the floor, fleetingly aware of an eerie, flickering hint of light, where burning oil from the smashed lamp rivuleted along the carpeting. She grappled with Polhaus, fighting as Harrigan had for possession of the revolver.

But Jessie was no match for Polhaus's muscular strength, and she was viciously backhanded, then rocked loose by a swiping uppercut. She kicked out savagely but groggily for Polhaus's groin, her boot taking the rancher with a glancing blow on his thigh. He wobbled, once again unable to train his revolver accurately—and Harrigan, recovering, tackled him, and they both went down, splintering a chair.

Jessie stepped back a pace, trying to clear her ringing head. She now became fully conscious of the flames tonguing upward from the base of the wall, igniting the varnished wood paneling. It was then, too, that she first heard the shouting of men's voices out in the yard, drawn by the shots and the beginning tendrils of fire. If they came in before she and Harrigan could get out—

Alarmed, Jessie moved in on the two men wrestling on the smoldering carpet. Harrigan was groping desperately for the pistol again, while Polhaus was struggling and swearing, punching and chopping with his feet, fists, and gun. Jessie picked up a broken chair leg and struck Polhaus hard, feeling yielding flesh and cartilage as blood spurted hot and wet from the rancher's mashed nose.

Fire had seized on the heavy drapes by now, and was flowing up toward the ceiling. Gagging and choking, Harrigan hauled Polhaus upright to land the final punch. But Polhaus, half-blinded and spluttering in agony, continued to fight like a man possessed. His pistol barrel struck Harrigan a glancing blow in the throat. Harrigan thrust him away, wavering groggily as Polhaus caromed into a burning sideboard and rebounded into the thick of the fire.

Smoke swirled, stinging their throats to rawness. Polhaus was held for an anguished moment in a lurching paroxysm. "Damn you!" His voice was a bleating scream. "Damn you!" Then heat and smoke caught at him, oily flames consuming his clothes and flesh.

Jessie and Harrigan lunged for the windows. They were locked, and impatiently Harrigan used his elbow to smash out the panes. Ruby sparks swirled about them, the room swiftly becoming the heart of a raging furnace. Sliding outside, Jessie felt no twinge of remorse for the rancher left within; her sympathy was all directed toward Polhaus's victims, like the dead youth at the pool.

They headed away from the house, unseen by the ranch hands, who were rushing about futilely, trying to curb the fire. But the house was unsalvageable, its seasoned timbers snapping and crackling, acrid smoke roiling from its eaves and roof sheathing.

"This way," Jessie urged, "to the corral."

It was, she figured, the best of bad choices. Returning to the claybank would be foolish, since they needed two horses; and it would be hazardous, there being too much open ground to cross.

Jessie led the limping Harrigan past the rear of some of the outbuildings, cautiously skirting the open yards. Brush tearing at their limbs and clothing, they forged through to the bank of the creek, where, unhesitating, they plunged in. The stream was more syrupy mud than flowing water, but they slogged across it and, grasping roots and branches for handholds, climbed the opposite bank.

Reaching the corral, they slipped between the fence-rails. A dozen or so horses milled restlessly in the enclosure, turned skittish by the blaze and resultant commotion. They managed to calm a couple of the animals, and Harrigan even found halters for them, draped carelessly in a bunch along one fencerail. They had led their horses out a side gate in the fence, and were mounting them bareback when two figures rode out from concealing rocks.

"Jessie!"

There was relief in Ki's voice, and relief in Jessie's too, as she and Harrigan hastened to join him and Evita.

"Ki, but how—?"

"We saw you running from the house," Evita answered for him.

And Ki, regarding Harrigan, asked, "How'd you get here?"

"Polhaus had me snatched, so he could—" Harrigan paused, his voice drowned out by the raucous shouts and pounding hooves of the eight riders swarming into the ranchyard. "I'll explain later, Ki!"

Evita, wheeling her horse, said loudly, "If we cut northwest from here, we'll run into the ranch road to Mosquero, *de acuerdo?*"

"Muy bien," Jessie responded.

Together, the four galloped toward the craggy rises beyond the ranch. Jessie glanced back once. The ranchyard was boiling with dust and confusion, the area lit eerily by the torch that had been August Polhaus's luxurious home, and was now his expensive bier.

When shortly they intercepted the ranch road, Ki called a halt to trade horses with Harrigan. The pinto was the only saddled mount, and despite Harrigan's protests that his wound wasn't bothering him, he finally accepted the saddle's extra support and comfort for his leg.

They rode on, hard and in silence. Harrigan was a fine horseman; despite his weakened condition, there was no problem along those lines. Nor was there any problem with pursuit. Even if Polhaus's gunhands were to try, there was little chance they could overtake them, or would keep up the chase as far as Mosquero. Jessie and Ki had known others like those men, and figured the odds were that once Polhaus was discovered dead, his crew would disband and scatter to the winds.

The first time they slowed to give their horses a breather, they began relating their various experiences—except for some judicious editing of more personal incidents that had occurred. Harrigan expressed shock at the news of De Baca's duplicity, and outright horror at the plan to blow up the congressional train at Purgatory Gorge.

"We can't let it happen," he declared. "De Baca may be a maniac, but he's right—he'll start a war between us and Mexico."

"It won't happen," Jessie assured him. "If we aren't delayed anymore, we should be able to get to Mosquero in time to wire ahead."

"I pray you're right, Jessie," Harrigan said grimly.

They rode with steady determination through the night.

Eventually the waning strength of their horses forced

them to slow considerably, even to stop a few times and take rest breaks. At last the darkness of the night began to dissipate, the pearly gray of predawn spreading along the eastern skyline; in the distance Mosquero emerged as a clump of pale, square edges that distinguished it from the surrounding countryside. By this time they were approaching it at little more than a walk.

Evita managed a weary smile when she glimpsed the town on the horizon. "We have made it!" she exulted.

Ki gave the girl a smile. Jessie leaned forward to rub her horse's neck. Harrigan straightened in the saddle as they continued across the final stretch of mesquite and cactus and greasewood. The sun climbed slowly, reddish streamers thrusting above a jumble of upended terrain into the cloudless blue.

It was bright morning and growing hot when the four entered the town. They were observed by early-rising townsfolk as they rode along the dusty main street, and by the time they reached the sheriff's office, a small crowd had begun to gather around them.

As they were dismounting, the office door opened and Sheriff Ballard came out. "What in tarnation! I'm seein' ghosts!"

"Almost, Sheriff, almost." Quickly and tersely, Jessie explained much of what had happened since they'd seemingly disappeared into thin air. There were gasps of shock and dismay from the crowd, and Ballard scowled with mounting anger.

When she was through, Ki spoke up. "We've got to send a telegram to the depot at Deming, so the train can be stopped—"

151

"Can't, m'boy!" a voice interrupted. The redheaded telegrapher stepped forward. "The line's dead 'twixt here and there. Sorry."

Ki swore. "Since when?"

"I dunno. Since before I woke up and opened for business."

"Since last night," Jessie said, sighing. "That bunch who chased us down out of the mountain camp, I bet. When they realized we'd slipped them, they must've hightailed it straight to the gorge."

"And De Baca, figuring out what we'd try to do, cut the wire. Or that bunch figured it out first, and cut it before reporting to him." Ki turned to the telegrapher. "Where can you send to?"

"Nowhere."

"Von Eismann." Jessie shook her head. "The Iceman's thorough; he'd make sure we couldn't relay our message to Deming in a loop."

"An' the nearest town for sendin' is Deming," the telegrapher added. "Which don't do us a lick of good."

Jessie ran a hand across her dusty face. She looked as exhausted as she felt, but her eyes glowed under their sunburned lids. "There's got to be a way. How far is Purgatory Gorge from here?"

"Too far to get to afore the train," Ballard replied.

"You sure?"

"Sure, I'm sure! Calc'late it for yourself. The train is supposed to pull out of Deming in about an hour, and I doubt that a train fulla Washington bigwigs will be behind schedule. It'll take it three hours at the most to reach the gorge. It'll take us five hours to ride there, at least five, and I mean leaving fresh and pushing the whole while."

"But we can't simply do nothing!" Harrigan argued. "No matter how impossible it seems, we can't give up. We have to try something!"

"We'll try. I don't know how or what, but we'll try." Ki lapsed quiet for a moment, thinking hard, then glanced at Jessie as an idea struck him. "Do you remember the train ride coming here?"

"Yes. Why?"

"Didn't we pass a little trainyard at the edge of town, and wasn't there a switch engine or something like that on a siding?"

"You're right, Ki!" Heartened, Jessie asked the sheriff, "Who's in charge of the trainyard? We need that engine!"

"But it's a relic, Miss Starbuck! It's got more patches on its boiler than I've got on my coffeepot! It'll . . ." Ballard hesitated, swallowing, while around him the crowd murmured excitedly. Then he nodded. "By gum, if it did hold together, it could make the gorge in time, maybe. Hitch on a car or two, and we'd give 'em hell!"

"Well, if we're going to spring that trap in time, we'll have to move fast," Jessie said. "How soon can we leave?"

"Soon's we get that little pufferbilly fired up," Ballard said. He turned to the crowd, calling out, "We need some able-bodied men! Who's game to go?"

The response of the townsfolk and cowboys was immediate and vociferous. They'd been spoiling for a chance to strike back at the murdering raiders who'd been spreading so much terror and destruction across the territory, and now their chance had come. They swarmed closer, loudly volunteering their services as

153

many of them had before, after the Renegaders' massacre at La Posada Duquesa.

"Grab your weapons and ammunition," Ballard ordered stoutly. "Meet us at the railyard as quick as you can. Now get crackin'!"

The men raced away, leaving only a few women and elders standing around. Harrigan rubbed his hands along his trouser legs, and said to Sheriff Ballard, "If you've got a spare rifle, I'll come along too."

Jessie took his arm. "You're going to bed."

"Whoa up, I want to be—"

"I know you want to, Victor. But you're in no shape to. You need to rest and doctor that leg, or it's going to fester."

Harrigan started to bluster, but now Ki had him by his other arm, and he was gently yet firmly steered up the street to the hotel. Evita walked with them; she was tired, though her eyes were bright and eager. When they entered the lobby, Jessie stopped and said to her, "Now tuck him in, Evita, and make sure he stays put this time."

Harrigan chuckled. "I'll keep my window locked."

Evita frowned. "You don't wish me along?"

"I wish you to keep an eye on Mr. Harrigan," Jessie answered.

"Don Felipe murdered my father, " Evita said. "Can you deny me the chance to kill him? Or at least to watch him die?"

"I can, and I am. Your people need you, Evita, just as our people need Mr. Harrigan. You mustn't risk your life for mere revenge."

Evita tried to argue, but Jessie and Ki both were adamantly determined to keep her out of harm's way.

154

Perhaps Jessie's explanation was a tad flowery; perhaps Evita wasn't quite as indispensible to Mexico as Jessie had said. But there was no question that there would be warfare at Purgatory Gorge; it was certain that there'd be shooting, and that there'd be casualties. Evita wasn't to be one of them.

It took some doing, but she finally agreed to remain behind.

Jessie and Ki left for the railyard. Arriving, they found Sheriff Ballard deep in conversation with an elderly, rotund man named Metzenbaum. He was a retired engineer and part-time superintendent of the yard, and Ballard had conscripted him. From the look on Metzenbaum's face, his arm hadn't needed twisting for him to agree.

Several other men were already in the yard, some of them talking in small groups, others coupling a spare passenger coach to the fuel bunker mounted behind the cab of the 0-4-0 saddletank switch engine. The boiler had been fired, and steam chuffed out of the engine's stovepipe stack. Its rhythm sounded weak to Jessica, but Metzenbaum assured her that it was sturdy and dependable. It had counterbalanced wheels, he told her, to minimize "hammer-blow" on the tracks, and big sandboxes to assist track friction. Best of all, he bragged, the water tank draped over the boiler, allowing it to travel quite a ways without needing a refill. This switcher would get them to Purgatory Gorge, he guaranteed it.

Jessie took Metzenbaum's guarantee with the grain of salt it merited, but said nothing. She merely nodded and turned to help Sheriff Ballard and Ki round up the assembling men and herd them into the coach.

When everyone was more or less in place, Jessie counted a total of twenty-three men. Hardly an army, but enough to hold their own against De Baca and his gang of killers—she hoped.

Minutes later, the wheezy old switch engine shuddered into motion, rods grinding and wheels flashing, its boiler sounding as though it were about to explode.

★

Chapter 11

Sunlight flamed at them from the western sky, gilding the tracks before the onrushing switch engine. Inside the cab, Ki squinted as the sun fired the glass windscreen set at an angle outside the open side window. There was sweat on his bare back, mixed with soot; he had shed his shirt and vest, and was helping the fireman, a man whose name he never did learn, to shovel crumbly coal into the firebox. The heat inside the cab was intense, much hotter than the desert sun had been during yesterday's endless riding.

After the train had crossed an expanse of upland plains west of Mosquero, the terrain had begun to roughen with jagged rock formations, and the right-of-way had become narrower and more winding. Now thick brush on steep slopes hemmed in the speeding, one-car train.

At the throttle, Metzenbaum puffed furiously on a stubby clay pipe, and alternated between checking the tracks and watching the pressure gauge. The fireman had his eye on the gauge too; he acted much less sanguine about the readings than Metzenbaum did.

"Hope she don't blow," he told Ki, his face long and soulful, like a basset hound's. "This's only a shuttle, y'know, and was boneyarded out to us at Mosquero when the railroad gave up fixing it."

Metzenbaum overheard that. "Bullshit," he declared, and tapped the gauge. The needle wavered uncertainly. "She'll take plenty more."

"The coal's lousy too," the fireman grumbled, shoveling.

As though to prove his point, Metzenbaum hooked the reverse bar another notch and widened the throttle. The whir of drivers, the pulse of cylinders, the blast of the exhaust created a thunderous din. Metzenbaum added to the racket by pulling on the whistle cord; a shrill scream echoed from the tube on the second boiler hump. He tugged the cord again, and then a third time. Ki could only think it was because Metzenbaum was recalling the highballing days of his youth and enjoyed the piercing sound of the whistle. There was definitely nothing on or around the tracks that needed to be signaled.

Ki picked up his shovel and dipped into the bunker for another load of coal. Space was cramped in the tiny cab, and the air was clogged with cinders and smoke as the switcher, its wheel flanges protesting, surged on up into the foothills bordering the Florida Mountains. Ki kept on shoveling, sweating, his muscles aching with strain and fatigue. He was in his second day with no sleep and precious little rest, and he knew he was going to have to pack it in pretty soon. Otherwise, neither his mind nor his reflexes would be functioning worth a damn when the train reached Purgatory Gorge.

Purgatory Gorge . . . and Von Eismann. This time the diabolical Prussian assassin would not escape; this time, Ki vowed, no trickery would prevent his capture or, preferably, his death. It was odd, Ki thought; samurai discipline was based on codes of honor and loyalty, yet combat depended on objective dispassion. But when it came to Von Eismann, Ki felt as though he'd hated the cartel's hired killer even before he knew he existed—hated what the Iceman was, at least, if not precisely who.

The tracks began to thread through the first of the high-country valleys, between scalloped rock crevices and terraced, wooded slopes. Filtered by the trees, the sun made shiny ribbons of the rails ahead, cast light into the brush-laden gullies and along the sheer stone banks that flanked the right-of-way. Ki grew increasingly sluggish, his arms feeling as if lead weights were attached, dragging them down.

The fireman clucked his tongue. "You sure do look peaked. Go on, crap out a spell. I can handle this chore m'self, honest."

Metzenbaum nodded agreement. "He has been for years."

"All right, but wake me if I oversleep," Ki said, laying aside his shovel. "I want to be up here in the cab when we hit the gorge."

"Sure, I'll give you a toot."

"Thanks." Ki scrambled across the fuel bunker and let himself down on the small platform behind it. There was little room, and the train rolled and pitched, the pin-couplers twisting erratically in a backlashing motion. Ki held on to the deck brace, judging the leap.

He sprang as the switcher and the coach tilted the same way. His slippered feet hit the duckboard walkway, and his hands tightened around an iron rung of the ladder leading to the roof. He firmed his hold, then opened the door and stepped inside the car.

The interior was stifling warm with humanity, yet relatively quiet. The pitching motion created dancing patterns of sunlight and shadow on the faces of the men sitting in the hardback bench seats. When they talked, their voices were low and determined, and rarely did they budge, their rifles, carbines, and an occasional shotgun propped upright between their legs. They glanced up at Ki as he swayed past; some nodded, others smiled coolly, but all were stern with resolution.

He squeezed in beside Jessie and Sheriff Ballard, who were sitting on a bench next to a cold potbellied stove. "Everything okay?" Ballard asked, shifting to make room. "No blowouts?"

"So far both engine and crew are holding pressure."

Jessie smiled. "How much longer at this rate?"

Ballard extracted a large silver watch from his vest pocket. "Reckon an hour an' a half, two hours."

"If we're lucky, De Baca and his pals won't be entirely set up. Then we'll be able to stop the train on the other side of the trestle."

"Don't tell them that." Ballard jerked his chin toward the other men. "They'd be plumb disappointed not to settle a few accounts."

"They'll get their chance," Jessie said. "Sooner or later."

Ki yawned, and slumped to take a catnap. It was more difficult to sleep than he'd thought; visions swirled through his mind of the politicos unwittingly rushing to their doom, of De Baca and his cutthroats ruling Mexico, of Von Eismann's criminal bosses ruling De Baca, and mostly of the coachful of men on whose luck and prowess the fate of two countries lay.

These were plain, everyday folk, the average citizens who would help build New Mexico into a territory and who would one day make it a state. Evita's father had been wrong, very wrong, when he'd accused the *anglos* of having grown soft. The men in this coach, Ki thought, were hardier and more courageous, resilient, and unflinching than any other population in the history of the world—including the samurai, who were a picked elite, set above the masses and acknowledged to be superior to them. What made the difference here was that these uncommon men were the common man.

Ki dozed fitfully, but when a whistle blast from the cab woke him, he felt refreshed and alert. Jessie was leaning against the window, deep in slumber; Ki didn't wake her, but nodded to Ballard and walked back up through the car, working the stiffness out of his cramped muscles. He was hungry and preferred to be; fighting on an empty stomach made him appreciate his next meal all that much more.

Returning to the cab, Ki relieved the tired and soot-blackened fireman. "Coupla miles more, maybe," the fireman said. "We're high and still climbing."

There was a crispness to the air now, and a definite alpine look to the terrain. Ki could hear the valves popping and cracking, the old cylinders huffing like bagpipe bellows as the engine labored up the snaking grades. He watched Metzenbaum close the steam a little to relieve some of the boiler pressure, diminishing most of the noise.

Shortly they topped the grade and started winding along the rim of a canyon. On their left the slope was sheer, with bouldered ledges; on their right the rock face was less steeply angled.

The fireman yelled, "The gorge is comin' up!"

Ahead, the tracks swept into a long curve. Metzenbaum kicked the brakes lightly as they surged into it, then kicked them off again. Surrounding them was desolate beauty, a soaring chain of giant spires and naked stone that glistened almost wetly in the blazing sun.

The slopes steepened on both sides as they broached a defile. Then, swiftly, the terrain leveled out into a small plateau—a ledge that projected over the now dizzying depths of the canyon.

Purgatory Gorge.

The trestle loomed before them, a spindly crosshatching of wooden beams that looked like a fragile spiderweb linking the two sides of the chasm. The trestle curved slightly to give its length greater rigidity against the heavy winter winds and snows.

"Looks like it's made of toothpicks," Metzenbaum said.

Whatever else the engineer was going to say was lost. He cried out suddenly, wheeling and falling away from the throttle. Ki caught him, saw blood welling on his shoulder, and at the same time heard the faint, echoing crack of a rifle above the pounding of the engine. There were more cracks; bullets slapped against the boiler and sideplates, pinging off the thick iron, splintering the wooden trim.

"Down!" Ki yelled to the fireman.

The fireman hit the deck of the cab, facedown, arms folded tightly over his head. Ki hunkered as low as he could over the fallen Metzenbaum. Wonderful. They'd won the race against time, in the sense that they'd reached Purgatory Gorge ahead of the congressional party; but they'd lost what might prove to be the critical part of the race, just as Ki had been afraid they might. De Baca and his killers were already prepared, positioned in the rocks above. So the train couldn't stop; it'd be a sitting target. But the train couldn't continue; the trestle was booby-trapped with dynamite.

Ki made an instantaneous decision, based on instinct and on what he'd seen at De Baca's camp. What it boiled down to was that he'd rather fight here, and take some of the bastards along, than trundle out onto the wooden span and hope the other train heard the explosion.

Straightening, he leaped for the controls, slamming the throttle and reverse bar in, twisting the brake handle, and "wiping the gauges." The brake shoes ground against the wheels, causing the engine and coach to buck crazily. The drivers locked tight, sliding along the rails.

Metzenbaum raised himself on one hip. "What're you doing?" he cried.

"Stopping."

"Are you barmy? They're shooting at us!"

"They'll blow us up, if we head over the trestle."

"M'gawd, hadn't thought of that—yeow!"

Ki flung the reverse bar over and opened the throttle. The engineer's startled cry was muffled in the sudden thunder of drivers spinning backwards, the engine shaking spasmodically. The screech of metal on metal lessened; the old switcher shimmied, seeming to want to stand on its nose. They ground to a shuddering halt, the beginning of the trestle only a hundred yards away.

Steam hissed mightily from the ancient boiler. Bullets spanged metallically off the thick plates, rico-cheting through the mountain vastness. The men in the coach were returning the fire, forcing De Baca's forces to remain hidden in the rocks. Yet everyone in the rain was effectively pinned down, unable to get away without being riddled by crossfire. They were trapped, helpless, with no way to warn or halt the approaching train. And once that other train reached the trestle and began to cross—

Ki crouched by the cab entrance on his right, near the controls, and triggered Metzenbaum's revolver twice at a face up in the rocks. Both bullets, hurried as they were, from a weapon Ki was unused to, went low and only sent showers of grit spraying over the man. On the opposite side of the cab, the fireman was cursing a blue streak while firing a Springfield car-bine. Ki adjusted for his third shot, and the man threw up his hands and toppled out of the rocks.

Continuous gunfire shattered the day. While Ki was hunkering to reload from Metzenbaum's cartridge belt, he heard the low, mournful wail of an approach-ing train whistle. A coldness gripped him as he lis-tened to the whistle's reverberations fading away; from their beat and clarity, he estimated that the train was no more than a mile from the gorge now. They wouldn't hear the gunfire until it was too late for the engineer to stop. Nor was there enough steam left in the switch-er's bullet-punctured boiler to whistle a sustained alarm. Nor was there anything the men here could do.

Or was there?

Ki's mind whirled, and spun up an idea. He shouted across to the fireman, "Start heaving coal into the firebox! We've got to get the pressure up—somehow—even if the boiler's a sieve!"

"What'n hell for?"

"Didn't you hear that whistle? The special train's coming, and the only way to stop it from being blown up is to blow up the trestle first, in time for them to hear the explosion and brake."

Metzenbaum snorted. "Now I know you're barmy! You told us—"

"That we couldn't head over the trestle—we, our train. But I can, alone, in just the switch engine. What else can we do?"

The wounded engineer and the fireman were gaping, neither of them moving for two or three seconds. Then the fireman hefted his shovel. "You want pressure? Wal, damn your eyes, you'll get pressure!"

Ki hesitated until there was a momentary lull in the shooting, then burrowed up across the fuel bunker again and yelled loudly, "Ballard! Sheriff Ballard! Open the door so I can talk to you!"

Within a minute the connecting door opened, and Jessie stood in its shadows. "Ballard got winged in his . . . well, let's just say it's more comfy for him to lie on his stomach than to walk around. What's up?"

"I'm going to uncouple us, and I'll need covering fire."

"Ki? Is this another of your wild schemes?"

"No time now to explain. I need that cover, Jessie!"

"Done."

The door shut. Evidently it took a few minutes for Jessie to pass the instruction; there was a lengthy hush, like the calm before the storm, and then from both series of coach windows blossomed twin broadsides. While the barrages were at their withering peak, Ki dropped to the pin-coupler that connected the engine and the coach.

Feverishly, Ki dug at the fastenings of the pin, loosening it, trying to pull it free. Two slugs whined off the bunker; a third cut a buzzing path past his bowed head. He paid it no mind. He could still hear, above the gunfire, the wail of the other train whistle.

More bullets zipped by him, and there were shouts from the men inside the coach as they sent round after round up into the flanking rocks. Behind Ki, in the engine cab, the fireman could be heard cursing as he scooped coal into the boiler, and Metzenbaum could be heard prompting the fireman to shovel more, faster. . . .

Finally, Ki managed to worm the pin free of the couplers. He flung it down, pivoted upward, and rolled back across the bunker into the cab. Lumps of sooty coal bounced out with him, clattering on the footboards. A bullet plucked at his forearm, stinging, but he scarcely felt it. He went to where Metzenbaum slumped against the cab wall, his left palm pressed against the hole in his right pectoral.

"How're we doing for pressure?"

"She'll move, but she won't break no speed records."

"That'll do. Here, let's get you out."

"Dammit, it's my shoulder that's busted, not my leg," Metzenbaum growled, but he didn't complain when Ki and the fireman helped him over the bunker to the rear platform. "Comin' across!" the fireman yelled. The men in the coach responded with a fresh fusillade of covering fire, while the fireman and Metzenbaum hustled across and into the coach.

Ki scrambled back over the bunker to the cab, hearing the oncoming train whistle again. If his judgment was correct, it was now less than a half-mile from the gorge, and climbing fast. He released the brakes, yanked the throttle open. The worn-out switcher began to edge forward, drivers clanking, steam hissing from holes in the boiler. More bullets whanged off its metal hide as De Baca and his crew realized what was happening. But Ki kept down and stayed at the throttle.

The switcher seemed to inch along, even though he had the throttle wide open. The stuttering clamor of the valves and the staccato drumming of the exhaust swelled in his ears, but the needle in the pressure gauge wavered depressingly low. Ki started shoveling coal, feeding the firebox. The cowcatcher eased slowly onto the trestle. He could see the sheer rock walls of Purgatory Gorge, the dizzying drop to the depths below, and knew that unless he wanted that chasm to be his final resting place, he'd better think about jumping soon.

Working rapidly, he managed to jam his shovel between the throttle and the side guard, wedging it tight so that it wouldn't close automatically when he jumped, and halt the engine. After inspecting to make sure the shovel couldn't pop loose, Ki crawled over the bunker for what he hoped would be his last time. He poised on the thin platform as the engine nosed onto the trestle—

Then he leaped out to the side, away from the precipice but onto unprotected open ground—straight into the murderous fire from De Baca's men in the rocks above. He landed in a swift, rolling somersault, bullets gouging the earth around him as he rose up in a long dive for cover. He slid behind the first boulder, then pitched himself deeper into a slim crevice between two others, conscious of stinging pain in his arms and legs from rock cuts during his fall and roll.

For the moment he ignored the lead chipping splinters from the stone around him, concentrating instead on watching the switcher chug snaillike along the steel rails and wooden struts. Peripherally he glimpsed the stationary passenger coach, from which Jessie and the men from Mosquero were still sending heavy fire up into the slopes. It had been their relentless volleys that had allowed him to escape unharmed from the engine, pinning down the killers and upsetting their aim.

Again came the keening wail of the approaching train, so close that Ki knew it was just beyond the curve of the opposite ridge. As he peered across the gorge, he saw the advancing plume of smoke from its stack. Any second now, the locomotive would steam into view.

Breathlessly, Ki brought his eyes back to the switcher coasting along the trestle—just in time to see the explosion.

There was an earsplitting concussion, a blinding flash of orange light and acrid black smoke. Flying bridge particles and engine sections erupted through the flame and smoke, metal shards and coal briquets raining down all around.

The fireball that engulfed the switcher licked hungrily at the broken, teetering wreck that had once been the trestle. Then Ki, safe in his niche behind the boulder, saw what was left of the old engine fall end over end, trailing fire, toward the bed of the gorge.

As the last rumble of the explosion faded, there came the sound of two long and rather hysterical whistle blasts from the other train. Then its locomotive— a grand old Baldwin 2-6-0 "Mogul"—hove into view around the far bend, sparks flying from its wheel flanges as its engineer, having heard the explosion and now able to see what had happened to the trestle, applied full brakes. The cars and coaches behind it swayed violently, the tortured squeal of locking brakes and grinding metal reverberating off the cliff walls.

More of the burning trestle crumbled and followed the debris into the chasm. The last remaining timbers were disintegrating, just as an arch with its capstone missing will collapse. The onrushing locomotive skidded toward the brink, and for an instant Ki thought it would slide off the twisted rails at the edge and plunge downward, carrying its string of cars with it. But then he saw it shudder like a huge animal shaking itself, and tremble to a stop no more than a dozen yards from the gorge. Relief surged inside him as he watched smoke belch from the Mogul's diamond stack, blanketing the coaches behind it in sooty wreaths, the train slowly reversing from the gaping maw.

In the ranks of De Baca's killers, mass confusion seemed to have taken over. They were no longer shooting at the Mosquero posse, and Jessie and the men burst from the coach with weapons blazing, sensing that the tide of battle had turned in their favor. A half-dozen of De Baca's gun crew spilled out, dead or wounded, from their positions above, and the others suddenly seemed loath to stand and fight. There was only sporadic answering fire as the possemen, fanning

169

out on both sides of the tracks, made it to cover without a single casualty.

Jessie, hunching behind a melon-shaped boulder next to the slope, was reloading the pistol she'd been lent by Sheriff Ballard, when she heard a sudden, angry bellow. She recognized the voice as De Baca's—a voice maddened with rage and frustration.

"Attack!" De Baca was shouting from high in the rocks above Jessie. "Run the gringos into the gorge! We still outnumber them, you *crétinos!*"

His gang responded sluggishly; now it was the gringos who were on the attack, and it was plain that gringos could savor the sweetness of victory and revenge. De Baca's gunnies floundered. Then those who were still alive scattered in retreat, disobeying their *caudillo* as they fled for their horses or into the hills.

Jessie and the men from Mosquero shot down more of them, giving De Baca's men the same mercy that they themselves had shown the people of the villages they'd sacked and destroyed. The posse began to give chase, swarming from concealment and climbing up among the outcroppings on both sides of the tracks. None of De Baca's crew stood to face the onslaught. Jessie ran up into the rocks toward the place where she'd heard De Baca yelling . . . but De Baca was no longer there. Sharp-eyed and watchful, she searched the rocks and jackpines along the ridge.

Nothing.

Jessie was about to turn back when the noise of a small gravel slide brought her pivoting to her left. It was just some small bits of shale trickling down a steep bank, but gazing upward to its source, she made out the outline of De Baca, scrambling for the rim of the slope.

She called out, "You're through, De Baca, *finito!*"

De Baca's response was a pistol shot that went wide.

Jessie ducked anyway, swearing. De Baca had a short yet crucial head start, up a hill that would leave her perilously exposed. But she had to pursue, to stop him before he could crest the ridge and disappear into the highland forests.

She started climbing after him. The footing in the shale was negligible. She could see De Baca above her, hiking steadily, and chanced a shot. It hit close enough for him to react, jerking, then turning to fire again.

Jessie dropped flat, hugging the incline. Lifting her head, she saw De Baca moving again, so she got to her feet and thrust upward. The sharp rock slashed at her denims and bit into the flesh of her hands. De Baca fired a third time, once more forcing her down.

When she began edging higher again, Jessie perceived that De Baca was slowing, age and his luxurious style of living having sapped his vitality. But he'd still beat her to the rim at this rate, she realized. In a desperate attempt to catch up, she straightened and skittered in a loping run diagonally across to a more solid outcrop of stone. De Baca fired, but didn't come close. She began to climb in earnest now, clawing for boulders and drawing up between them, only to reach to grasp another, the broken shale still sliding out from beneath her feet if she put too much weight on it.

De Baca paused to squat and reload. Jessie used his delay to wriggle up another ten feet. De Baca aimed by the noise of the gravel slewing down from her grappling climb. His bullet clipped the rock next to her left hand, spitting tiny slivers of stone into her face. She could taste the blood oozing from the myriad tiny cuts, but refused to waste time wiping her face. She groped for the next highest rock, then the next, until, gasping, she reached the crest.

For just a moment she bent, hands on her knees, regaining her breath. Then she darted along the ridge rim toward the area where De Baca was likely to appear. She slewed around a small thicket of brambles, almost losing her balance again as her boots slipped in that treacherous shale. De Baca was stumbling over the edge, one hand clutching for support, any support, while the other held his revolver. They saw each other almost simultaneously.

"You!" De Baca snarled. "If it hadn't been for you—"

"It would've been someone else. And it wasn't only me, De Baca."

"True. You had a *japonés,* a handful of gringo *peones,* and a traitorous *puta.*" De Baca lumbered slowly toward her, his revolver leveled directly at her belly. But that was all right; Jessie had Sheriff Ballard's Colt aimed at De Baca's gut, too, "Bah! They were all traitors! I was betrayed, deserted! You saw how my cowards fled."

"Rats leaving a sinking ship. Your killing days are over."

"Not quite yet, Señorita Starbuck!"

De Baca fired with the speed of a striking rattler. But Jessie had been watching for those telltale signs in the eyes, in the mannerisms, and caught his mirrored reflex even before his finger completed its move. She sprang aside, De Baca's bullet grazing her jacket sleeve. Her pistol spoke once, and more to the point.

De Baca twisted, his second shot blowing a hole in his own boot. Jessie fired again as well, catching De Baca in the top of his skull as he fell forward, unable to balance on his remaining foot. He dropped, lifeless.

Meanwhile, Ki had joined some of the Mosquero possemen in pursuit of De Baca's gunhands. When they crested the rocks on the slope opposite Jessie, they saw that the gunmen there had gathered their horses and were scattering without discipline, without cohesion. They had neither the driving patriotism of Cardenas and Evita Torres, nor the determination of the outnumbered *anglos* who'd bested them; easy money is a fine cause, so long as it remains easy.

The men of the posse didn't pursue them any further. It would only be a matter of time before the stragglers were rounded up, on this side of the border or in Mexico. Starting back toward the railroad coach, Ki couldn't help wondering what had happened to Von Eismann. Had he been along? And if not, why not? If he had been, had he been one of those who'd escaped on horseback?

Ki wandered from the group, searching for an answer that would satisfy him. He scrambled upward through windswept firs to a knoll, thinking that perhaps he'd be able to spot some clue from the summit. When he reached it, he saw nothing, so he slid down the other side of the hill, figuring to work his way back around to the coach. At the bottom was a dark hollow, filled with bushes and saplings—one of the places where De Baca's gunhands had tethered their horses, since it connected at one end to the lip of the gorge, and at the other to a comparatively wide valley.

He had moved perhaps ten feet along the hollow when an eruption, a brilliant flash of fragmented light, fountained on his right. Bits of earth and splintered branches sprayed his lower body. The shock straightened him for an instant; then, reflexively, he dove into the hollow, rolling, squirreling along the ground.

Somebody was hidden out there. Somebody with a shotgun and an urge to kill. Ki lifted his right hand and eased it downward. His torso was bloody, but he sensed that the shotgun blast itself had missed him. He drew his *tanto,* wiped its slim, curved blade on his trouser leg, and gripped it tightly, waiting, watching, hearing the somebody stalking him, coming in to end it.

Concealed by rocks, leaves, and twigs, Ki lay motionless so as not to betray his position. His main chance was that the bushwhacker would be overconfident after that first, seemingly point-blank shot. It was difficult to see anyone lying still in a pocket of darkness, and Ki was counting on that, hoping for the element of surprise.

Then somebody came out of the thick brush of the hillside, a few feet below where Ki had been standing when he was hit. Von Eismann. In the metal claw of his false left hand he carried a leather briefcase, and in the same arm, cradled in his elbow, a single-barrel shotgun. In his right hand was a Webley-Pryse '76 revolver, held up and ready. His eyes ranged the brush. Ki hesitated, consciously restraining his driving desire to kill the Iceman, though it was sharp and painful in him.

Not yet . . . not quite yet . . .

Von Eismann half-turned away from him, and Ki realized that now—*now*—was the time to act. He rose and threw the knife.

His pitch was fluid and true. The blade flashed through the dimness and disappeared into Von Eismann's exposed right side, just below the ribs. His body stiffened in a rigid pose. Ki was already on his feet and rushing forward. He caught the haft of the knife just as Von Eismann began sagging in the middle. The blade came away cleanly. Von Eismann turned to face Ki, and there was pain but not astonishment in his glance. His briefcase and weapons dropped from his arms.

"Ach, was it poisoned?"

"My knife? No, no it wasn't."

"I'll recover then. *Gut."*

"What do you mean?" Ki demanded furiously. "You're dead!"

"Wounded." Von Eismann looked at his hand, which was clutching his injured side; there was fresh blood on his palm, but not much. "A jerkin, you see, I'm wearing a thick leather jerkin. Most uncomfortable in this climate, but I didn't trust De Baca either."

"A leather jerkin can't stop a .45 slug."

"No, but not all pistols are large caliber, nor shot from close range. A bullet may be slowed...or a knife partially deflected."

Ki regarded the knife in his hand, and rubbed his thumb along its blade. He glared at Von Eismann. Von Eismann read his thoughts.

"Mein freund, you won't kill me now."

"Don't count on it."

"I am your prisoner."

"If I were yours, you'd kill me."

Von Eismann tried to shrug, winced, and slowly sat down on the ground. "Maybe. But we live—and will die—by different codes."

Ki stared down at Von Eismann, feeling himself trembling. A little cut now, a two-inch slice, and the Iceman would be dead, and the pent-up rage within him would be relieved. Ki tried. He willed his hand to move, but it wouldn't. Von Eismann knew him too well.

"Damn you," Ki swore, and kicked the shotgun against Von Eismann's leg. "Go ahead, pick it up. Or the pistol; it's there too."

Von Eismann smiled, shaking his head.

"Then your false hand, the gun you've got hidden in its wrist. Try for it, damn you, try something!"

"Nein. I'm your prisoner."

Keeping one eye on Von Eismann, Ki knelt and pulled the dropped briefcase to him. Opening its catches, he examined its contents cursorily. Ledgers, handwritten notes, a folder of names: the sort of information Jessie needed to pursue her war against the cartel. He relatched the case and stood up, motioning to Von Eismann.

Slowly they trudged back to the railroad coach, Ki covering Von Eismann with the shotgun, the Webley stuck in his waistband.

If only I could kill him, Ki thought.

The Iceman, as though reading Ki's thoughts, said, "Don't worry. We'll meet again to decide our fates."

"I'm afraid not," Ki replied. "Not where you're going."

"We'll see, *mein freund . . .*"

Ki's only consolations were that Von Eismann would wind up rotting the better part of his remaining life in prison, and Jessie would wind up inheriting all of Von Eismann's records.

Meager comfort, though, in view of losing to the coldblooded Prussian.

Or perhaps not, Ki thought. Maybe the Iceman was right, and this was merely a temporary draw....

★

Chapter 12

With De Baca and his marauding gang vanquished, their Portrillo Mountain fort demolished, and Von Eismann awaiting trial at Santa Fe, the international conference in El Paso was almost an anticlimax. Yet it was the kind of anticlimax Jessie was proud to be a part of, and would have liked to see happen more often.

The congressional party arrived a couple of days after the fight at Purgatory Gorge, a bit worse for the stagecoach detour, but extremely pleased that the border conflict had been resolved. Good for America, they all said, not to mention good for the purpose of their political junket. After a few nights of investigating railroad practices in the clubs and salons of El Paso, they all decided to stay on through the conference, in order to add their wisdom and support. General Diaz dispatched a new, more trustworthy envoy, after being informed of De Baca's treachery. And the meeting became a goodwill exchange that helped foster closeness between the two countries.

Jessie and Ki were lauded for their bravery, as were Sheriff Ballard and the posse from Mosquero. Victor Harrigan also came in for his share of praise, though he was sorely distressed not to have been in on the skirmish at the gorge, and vowed that if and when there was a next time, he was going to be smack in the middle of it, come hell or high water.

As for *El Renegado*, whose followers still roamed the Mexican states of Sonora and Chihuahua, the subject was discreetly sidestepped at the conference. The Renegaders, as long as they remained on their own land south of the border, were of no concern to the United States. So, by tacit agreement, it was accepted that such internal problems of Mexico would be handled by Mexico without outside interference.

On the final night of the conference, there was a farewell party—one of those big, fancy shindigs where everyone wore boiled collars or hoop-skirted crinolines. Jessie attended as the guest of Representative Harrigan, although she knew personally just about all the dignitaries and politicians who were there.

Ki didn't go. He supposed he could have wangled an invitation, but getting duded up for a political hurrah was not his notion of a pleasant evening. He preferred doing what he was doing, lazing away the hours in a rowboat. More like a small skiff, actually, the Rio Grande not being overly wide or deep during the summer months. There was some pretty fair moonlight, and a soft night breeze; and the only sounds were filtering from the party, which was nearby at the river estate of the lieutenant governor of Texas.

And occasionally, a few sounds from Evita.

She'd accompanied Jessie and Ki to El Paso for no particular reason, other than that she had some thrice-removed relatives living there. Despite her earlier vow to unseat Diaz, no animosity had been shown either by her or by the new envoy from Mexico City. An unwritten truce had been posted, though Ki knew she would continue to do everything she could to better her people's lot—through peaceful means.

Evita was being very peaceful at the moment. She

179

was resting against the stern, wearing a new *camisa* and drawers, but nothing else. The way her long, supple legs were spread straight along the deck, her back arched and breasts thrust forward, and her gamine face tilted up, caressed by moonlight—that was exactly the evening's entertainment Ki enjoyed. It sure beat celluloid collars and whalebone corsets.

"Buenas noches." Evita smiled languidly.

"Buenas noches." Ki grinned back. "We're drifting."

"What a shame. And I've misplaced the oars."

"We'll hit shore eventually, in an hour or two."

"We'll be busy then. A rest now will do us good."

"A swim, though, would be refreshing."

"It has possibilities . . ."

Ki gazed across the turgidly flowing water, toward the terraced lawns where the farewell party was in full swing: sides of beef barbecuing over sagebrush pits; fiddle music and dancing; liveried waiters serving drinks and tugging forelocks; eloquent speakers outorating one another. The celebration, as Jessie had mentioned earlier to Ki, was expected to last far into the wee hours of the night.

Actually, Jessie had disclosed a bit more than that. The party was the first opportunity she'd have to be with Harrigan, the conference having kept him too busy for socializing. And she was rather concerned about him, as she'd divulged to Ki; all this excitement could be hard on Victor's leg, and she was worried that it might be bothering him. So after she and Harrigan ate together, danced together, Ki had a sneaking suspicion that they just might slip out somewhere quiet together, where together they could check that leg of his real well. . . .

Ki inhaled the sultry air and dug his toes into the deck. "Well, I don't know, Evita. Swimming could get us wet, you know."

"Oh, you're right." Evita stood and stretched, then snuggled over to put her arms tightly around his neck. "We'll have to keep as much of us dry as we can," she murmured. "Such as our clothes."

Her fingers plucked at the hem of his shirt, slowly digging it out from his waistband and then running her hands up along his chest.

"The excitement's over," Ki said. "You don't have to."

"I never did have to, Ki. Maybe the first time, but only right at first. And now—now I like to."

"And later, Evita? Tomorrow we go our separate ways."

"*Sí,*" she whispered sadly in his ear. "You have your world and I have mine, and neither of us will—or can—change for the other. But it's been nice. It still will be nice, until tomorrow."

"Ah, yes. The boat is drifting."

"And there is nothing we can do about it."

"Except enjoy it while we can." Ki kissed her, drawing her firm, resilient body to him.

He was wrong. The excitement wasn't over yet.

Watch for

LONE STAR AND THE BADLANDS WAR

sixteenth novel in the exciting
LONE STAR series from Jove

coming in November!